Terror
at TURTLE MOUNTAIN

Terror

at TURTLE MOUNTAIN

Penny Draper

This novel is a work of fiction. Names, characters, places, and incidents either are the product of the author's imagination or are used fictitiously. Any resemblance to actual persons, living or dead, is coincidental.

Edited by Barbara Sapergia.
Cover images: Photo of Edith P. Shaw, courtesty of Ben Parkinson.
Cover painting by Aries Cheung.
Cover design by Duncan Campbell.
Book design by Karen Steadman.
Printed and bound in Canada by Marquis Book Printing Inc.

Library and Archives Canada Cataloguing in Publication

Draper, Penny, 1957-
   Terror at Turtle Mountain / Penny Draper.

ISBN 1-55050-343-X

1. Frank (Alta.)--History--Landslide, 1903--Juvenile fiction.
I. Title.

PS8607.R36T47 2006   jC813'.6   C2006-901084-6

10 9 8 7 6 5 4 3 2

2517 Victoria Ave.
Regina, Saskatchewan
Canada   S4P 0T2

Available in Canada & the US from
Fitzhenry & Whiteside
195 Allstate Parkway
Markham, ON, L3R 4T8

The publisher gratefully acknowledges the financial support of its publishing program by: the Saskatchewan Arts Board, the Canada Council for the Arts, the Government of Canada through the Book Publishing Industry Development Program (BPIDP), Association for the Export of Canadian Books and the City of Regina Arts Commission.

For my mother
Meryl Grace Clapp
who lost her curls
when she got the measles

PROLOGUE

GRANDFATHER WAS SHOUTING. "IF YOU LEAVE my house with that man, you can never come back, so think well before you act. Look around you, daughter. Look at the life you are leaving, then imagine your life in a dirty coal town, married to a man who scrabbles for a living in the dark and the dust. Think about having that...that child...hanging on to your skirts for the rest of your life. Think about all the disappointment you have caused! Why can't you be more like your sister? She is a daughter of whom I can be proud."

Nathalie cowered behind her mother's long skirt. The dark, stuffy room her grandfather called the parlour frightened her. The faces of the portraits that hung on the walls seemed to glare at her, and the air had an old smell, as if dead things lived there. Even so, Grandfather was the most frightening thing in the room.

Nathalie was only three years old, but she was sure that she was "that child." Was she also "the disappointment"?

JUST THEN THE PARLOUR WALLS *began to swirl and mist, as they did every night. Nathalie fought her way up from the dream and was once more her thirteen-year-old self, curled next to her mother in their big bed. But the feeling remained — that pressure behind her eyes that made her unshed tears sting. For no matter how hard she tried, she was still that child. The disappointment.*

CHAPTER 1
Nathalie

NATHALIE ROLLED OVER IN BED TO CUDDLE her mother and share some of her warmth. It was such a cold morning for April. Judging from the temperature of the bedroom, Nathalie was sure she would have to wear her heavy winter boots to school yet again. How she hated those ugly boots.

Nathalie's mother gave her a quick hug, then got up and hurried to the kitchen. Nathalie sighed. "No time to lallygag," said her mother. "You've got milk duty."

Nathalie clutched the thin coverlet closer. Nathalie Vaughan on milk duty meant that Toby Wilkinson was on coal duty, and she would have to be alone in the school an hour early with him. Toby always made her do most of his chores, and teased her the whole time.

It was the duty of each family to provide coal for the stove for one week of the year. Most kids had fathers or big brothers who delivered the coal on a cart and helped their child start the stove before they went on to their own daily chores. Toby was so big his dad insisted that Toby do it himself, so there was never a grown-up around to make him work.

And Nathalie, of course, had no father or big brother at all. That was why her mother was exempt from coal duty, but in return Nathalie had to provide milk for the morning cocoa twice as often as the other kids. Her mother said they were lucky the school board had agreed to that arrangement, but as far as Nathalie was concerned, it was just one more thing that made her different from all the other kids with real families.

With a groan, Nathalie rolled from the bed, put on her slippers, and hurried to the kitchen. Her mother had the stove started and warmth was beginning to fill the tiny room. "I'm off," said her mother. Nathalie saw that her mom was already dressed for work. "In this cold, the washwater will take a while to warm up. Don't forget the milk."

And she was gone. Nathalie's shoulders slumped. She knew her mother's life was hard. Her job as housekeeper at the Imperial Hotel was demanding. Even so, it was hardly enough to make ends meet. But sometimes Nathalie wished that her mother wouldn't work quite so much, that she would sometimes stay at home and spend time with her daughter. It was bad enough that there were just the two of them. Sometimes she felt like an orphan.

Nathalie warmed up a square of porridge from the drawer, and drank the last of the tea in the pot. She pulled on her black woolen stockings backwards, making sure that the darned bit was behind her knee where nobody could see. Her blouse, skirt, and pinafore were clean and freshly pressed, as always. Her mother was always reminding her that she should feel lucky they were allowed to use the big hotel laundry to do up their clothes. It didn't matter much to Nathalie; there was so much coal dust in the air that she felt dirty all the time anyway.

She braided her hair, put on her coat, laced up the hated boots and fastened the two buckles at the top. With a deep sigh, Nathalie picked up the milk pail and turned towards the door. As she did, she caught a glimpse of her reflection in the kitchen window. Nathalie thought her nose was too small, her brown eyes too big, and her long dark hair too straight. She was too skinny by half. She wished, as she often did, that she looked more like her mother.

Nathalie believed her mother must have been beautiful as a girl. Caroline Vaughan was curvy in the right places, her hair was blonde and wavy, and her eyes were blue with little smile creases at the edges. Of course, the smile creases must have come from the time when Nathalie's father had been alive, as her mother rarely smiled now. If Nathalie could only have blonde hair and blue eyes, maybe she wouldn't always remind her mother of her father and her mother could be happier. Nathalie tried to push those thoughts to that place behind her eyes; that place where she kept her unshed tears. She had no room for them in her day. With another sigh, she jammed her tam over her dark braids and headed out to the hotel.

The sun was up, but it was hard to tell in the town of Frank. As Nathalie picked her way along the wooden sidewalk that led from her front door to Dominion Avenue, she surreptitiously glanced up at the reason why. Turtle Mountain stared right back at her. The town of Frank was nestled right at the foot of the mountain that blocked the light from the town.

Nathalie didn't like the mountain. It rose up behind the town, growing higher and higher until it cast a shadow over a good part of the valley below. Dominion Avenue, the main street of town, ran right into the mountain, and where it ended there was a door that led inside into the dark. It wasn't a door really, it was a mine shaft used by the men of Frank who made their living digging coal from deep inside the mountain.

Nathalie had seen the miners when they emerged from the mine, all covered in black dust. It always seemed to her that the mountain had swallowed them, then spit them back out, half chewed. To her, the mountain was a living thing, an ominous presence that shut out the light and ate the men. Her mother said that her imagination needed a little toning down. Still, Nathalie lifted her head a little higher when she turned the corner onto Dominion Avenue and could put Turtle Mountain at her back. That way, as she walked away from the mountain, she was walking towards the Canadian Pacific Railway train tracks at the opposite end of the street. It was fun to imagine the places the train might visit, much more fun than thinking about the confining darkness of the mountain.

Dominion Avenue was a wide, broad street that seemed to be full of activity at all hours of the day and night. As in most towns in the North-West Territories, the street was unpaved and often muddy, so Nathalie took care to stay on the wooden sidewalk, boots or no boots. At this hour of the morning, the proprietors of the many shops on Dominion Avenue were opening up for business, and there were knots of men chatting in front of the Alberta Mercantile and the Palm Restaurant. Nathalie passed D. J. McIntyre's Hall, which had a real piano for theatricals and doubled as the Methodist Church on Sundays. Further along was the Frank Dairy, where families with young children could get milk from the cow in the back yard. Nathalie waved to Mr. Cameron, who was dusting the sign over his small shop that read "Watchmaker and Marriage Licences," then stopped at the window of Crown Studios. Their sign said, "Our photographs will always whisper, Come Again."

Nathalie loved to look at the family portraits displayed in the window. She thought that the children in the photographs were saying, "Our photographs will always whisper, Let Us Out!" All the children looked so itchy in their best clothes, the women so serious, and the miners so clean! Nathalie knew every one of the people in the window and the difference between the photographs and real life made her smile. She wondered how different she might look in a photograph. Not so very much, most likely, as she and her mother probably looked as serious as the people in the photographs all of the time.

Further along was the tiny office of the Frank *Sentinel*, the local newspaper. Nathalie did not peer into this window, as Harry Matheson, the editor, either had a limited selection of type or was a very poor speller. Whatever the reason, the misspellings on the front page made the paper hard to decipher. Next came the drugstore, the bank, and Mr. Leitch's grocery and furniture store.

Nathalie crossed from one wooden sidewalk to another as Dominion Avenue crossed Fifth Street, just missing Mr. Beebe's horse and buggy as he made his laundry deliveries. The Imperial Hotel was on the corner. There were four hotels in Frank – the town was growing so quickly – but the Imperial was the biggest and the nicest, in Nathalie's opinion. It was made completely of wood, but unlike the other hotels it didn't need to have a false front to make it look more imposing. As she made her way around to the kitchen door at the back of the hotel, Nathalie felt very proud that her mother worked at the grandest hotel in Frank.

While the cook filled her milk pail, Nathalie strained to catch a glimpse of her mother, but she was nowhere to be seen, so Nathalie made her way down Fifth Street to the school. She sighed. It was time to do Toby's chores.

CHAPTER 2
Rolling Chalk

TOBY WAS ALREADY THERE, SHOVELLING COAL into the stove. "You're late!" he said. "I almost had to do it all myself."

"Toby," said Nathalie patiently, "you are *supposed* to do the stove yourself. It's your job this week."

"Not when I've got you to do it for me," Toby said with a grin. He sat down at a primary student's desk and put his big boots on another desk. The tiny chairs made him look even bigger that he was. He ran his huge hands through his black hair and leaned back in the tiny chair. "Now, Nattie, while you're finishing the fire, I need you to tell me about Samuel de Complain. I've got a history test today."

"It's Champlain, not Complain, you big oaf! Didn't you study?"

"Course not. On coal week, I've got you to help me every morning."

Nathalie just shook her head. It wasn't that she minded helping other students; being a Senior in a small school meant that a good part of every day was spent tutoring the little ones. But Toby wasn't little. He was just plain lazy. But because Nathalie did not have the courage to stand up to him, she finished the fire, put the milk on to heat, then went to the slate board to trace Champlain's explorations on the map of Canada, pointing out each step of the journey to Toby for his test.

Nathalie had Champlain in Port Royale when she heard Toby snoring. She whirled around in dismay, only to see her teacher standing at the door. Miss Ryaness must have been listening to Nathalie's lesson.

"You have more patience than I do," said Miss Ryaness with a smile. "I gave up trying to teach him that Champlain wasn't Complain ages ago."

Nathalie smiled shyly. Miss Ryaness had never spoken to her quite like that before, like a grown-up. "He makes me cross sometimes. But it's hard to say no when he asks for help," she replied.

"As I said, you have more patience than I. Would you mind rolling out some more chalk for me? There's very little left. I will wake up our sleeping beauty here."

"Of course not, Miss Ryaness," said Nathalie, giggling. Sleeping Beauty? Toby?

Nathalie went into the little lean-to attached to the back of the school that they used for supplies. She loved the new school. The coal mine was doing so well it had turned the tiny village of Frank into a busy town. Miners and their families were arriving every day, with more and more children registering at the school. Finally the school board had decided that they needed a larger building. Everyone in Frank had helped, and now they had this lovely building with two classrooms, a cloakroom for the boys and another for the girls, and a lean-to for supplies.

Nathalie wrestled a large bowl down from the shelf and measured out five pounds of plaster of Paris and one pound of flour. She got some water from the pump outside and mixed it all together. As she was kneading the mixture, Lester Johnson arrived.

"Miss Ryaness told me you were back here," he said. "Can I help?"

Nathalie was blushing so much she didn't dare lift her head. Her friends all thought that Lester was a pretty ordinary kid, but to Nathalie he was special. She didn't know why exactly. He wasn't the handsomest boy in the class, or the funniest, or the smartest. They had played together since they were little. But lately, if Lester walked into the schoolroom Nathalie felt somehow more alive, and looking forward to his arrival made the day more exciting. It wasn't as if they actually played together any more, or even talked much to each other. At least, not until today.

Nathalie rolled out the chalk and began to cut it into strips. Lester cut the strips into short lengths and both worked at rolling the pieces into even round sticks. Soon they heard Miss Ryaness start the Lord's Prayer. "We'd better get back," whispered Nathalie. "Um, thanks." And that was all she'd managed to say the whole time they'd worked together. As she took her seat, Nathalie mentally groaned at her witty conversation. She wished she didn't feel so shy with him.

After the Lord's Prayer and the singing of "God Save the King," Miss Ryaness addressed the class. "Today is Bounty Day," she said. "All of you with tails please bring them to the front to be counted." The North-West Territories had such a problem with gophers that they had placed a bounty on them. Many schoolchildren set traps and snares along their school routes, and teachers were given the task of counting the tails and paying the children. Nathalie and her best friend Frances thought the whole business was disgusting.

One by one the boys filed up. Albert had two, Carl Jr. one, and John Alexander three. Little Billy Warrington, who was only eight, proudly carried a pail to Miss Ryaness. "I've got six!" he exclaimed. Billy lifted the lid. A horrible smell filled the room. The Primary girls began to shriek, "What's that, Miss Ryaness?" The Senior girls held their noses, and the boys rolled with laughter.

"What's the matter?" asked Billy.

"You're only supposed to bring in the tail, not the whole gopher!" laughed Albert. "Don't you know anything?"

"Billy," asked Miss Ryaness, "how long ago did you trap these gophers?"

"Couple of weeks, Miss," replied Billy. "I wanted to get a good lot. And I did, didn't I?" he exclaimed proudly.

"You certainly did," said Miss Ryaness, whose face had gone quite green from the smell emanating from the pail. "Next time, Billy, please bring in just the tail and bring it in *right* after you catch it. Do you understand?"

"Yes, Miss. Can I have my money now?"

Miss Ryaness counted out the pennies, and Billy went proudly back to his seat. Miss Ryaness called Toby to the front. "Toby, since you're on chores this week, perhaps you would light a small fire down at the end of the lane and burn these unfortunate creatures. The rest of us would be grateful."

Toby picked up the offending pail and took it outside. It took some time for the class to settle down to their reading, so by recess little had been accomplished.

CHAPTER 3
The Rocky Mountain Ogre

THE TEMPERATURE HAD DROPPED EVEN FUR-
ther. The Senior girls decided to forego their
skipping ropes to stay inside and play tiddlywinks. Ruby Watkins was the school champion.
Nathalie could never figure out if it was because
Ruby's aim was true or because she was so competi-
tive. Nathalie never seemed to get her aim right and
sent counters all over the place. She never got them
into the cup. There was no doubt that she was smart
in her head, but Nathalie despaired of having any
smarts in her fingers. When it came to games that
required dexterity, she was always last. Her mother had
tried to teach her sewing many times, suggesting she
could help with the mending that brought in a little
extra money, but her results were always disappointing
and her mother finally gave up on her.

After recess came mathematics, and the class was quiet. The only sound was the scratching of chalk on slates. Nathalie concentrated on the sums on the board. The long columns of numbers were written in different colours, with each grade doing the problems of a certain colour.

She smiled to herself as she remembered her first day at school. She hadn't known about the colours and tried to do all the problems, right up to the Senior level. At lunch she had run away. She had run all the way down Fifth Street, past Dominion Avenue, farther and farther until she had reached the wooden bridge that linked the townsite with the miners' cabins on the other side of Gold Creek. Her mother had decreed that she was too little to go past the bridge, so she had hidden under it. All day she had huddled under the old timbers, wishing that she could be smart enough for school. She had cried for a while, felt lonely for a while, and then been distracted by the trickling water that was passing under the bridge. The noise it made was so cheerful that Nathalie had forgotten why she was sad.

It had been nightfall before anyone found her. Her mother had been so angry, and so upset. When Nathalie had finally told her why she had run away, she could tell that her mother didn't know whether to laugh or cry. Ever since then, Nathalie had kept her eye on the problems of the grade ahead and listened to their instructions. She knew that she didn't have to actually do those problems, but she wanted to be ready. Never again did she want to feel as foolish as she had in the first grade. And ever since then, Nathalie had loved the bridge over Gold Creek. Sadness was swept away by the cheerful water. It was a place where wishes could come true.

At lunchtime, Mr. Clapp, John's father, came to get his son out of school. Mr. Clapp worked the day shift at the mine doing maintenance on some of the equipment, and he liked to take John to the mine when an extra hand was needed. John was always happy to go. A job at the mine was the goal of most of the Frank boys and having a father who could show you the ropes was a lucky break.

Nathalie couldn't understand why anyone would want to work there. Even if she had been a boy, she couldn't imagine spending her life in the dark, filthy dirty. She had seen the state of the men's overalls when they came into the hotel. They were so stiff with coal dust that sometimes they could have stood up all by themselves. No, when Nathalie grew up she would have a neat and clean job where she could use her brain and not her hands.

As the children ate their lunches, the air was suddenly split by the sound of the afternoon passenger train. Maybe that was what she would do when she grew up, thought Nathalie. She would leave Frank and take a ride on the train to some exotic place where she would never see coal dust again. Actually, at thirteen years old, she would find just riding on the train excitement enough. Sometimes the kids would run after the trains as they left town to go back to Lethbridge, or on to the west coast. The brakemen who rode the caboose would encourage them, and the boys would see who could run farthest before the train moved out of sight. Sometimes the brakemen threw hard candy to the kids. Nathalie had watched, but never scrambled for the candy. She knew her mother would have disapproved.

In the afternoon the whole school practised penmanship. Jessie Leitch groaned all the way through the lesson. She found it terribly difficult to adjust her pen nib so that it wouldn't make splotches all over the page. Finally it was manual arts. The girls practised their feather stitch on old stained napkins donated by the hotel, and the boys worked with small tools in the schoolyard. Nathalie's feather stitches looked more like crow tracks. She just couldn't get her fingers to obey her mind. Frances tried to help. Frances was very good at sewing. She had to be; she had eight brothers and sisters and had been hemming diapers since she was a little girl. But even Frances couldn't get Nathalie's work untangled, and the two friends finally gave up.

Miss Ryaness looked up from her marking. "Nathalie, the little ones are nearly finished with their sewing cards. Will you tell them a story until I finish with these papers?"

NATHALIE WAS RELIEVED. Telling stories was much easier that making her stitches neat. She pulled her chair to the other side of the room and the Primaries put away their cards in anticipation.

"Tell us about a princess!" cried one little girl with ringlets.

"No, a monster!" yelled out Delbert Ennis. "A pussycat!" "A bear!" "My daddy!" others called out.

Nathalie laughed. "What kind of a story would that be? Let's pick three things, and we'll make the story about just those three."

Hands flew up all around her. Nathalie chose the hand that went up first. "We should have an ogre."

"All right, an ogre. Where does the ogre live?"

"Under a mountain!" Nathalie picked another hand. "Which mountain will the ogre live under? How about Turtle Mountain, just outside?"

"Oh no," cried a little girl in a blue pinafore. "That's right beside our town. I don't want an ogre living that close. I'll be too scared to come to school."

So it was decided that the ogre would live in the Rocky Mountains, far away from Frank. The children added a seamstress who made perfect stitches; they were clearly still thinking of their sewing cards. The children, with Nathalie's help, had the ogre leave his mountain with a great tumbling of rocks. He decided to come to Frank, much to the horror of the little girl in the blue pinny. After some adventure the seamstress sewed his trouser legs together so that he couldn't get to Frank after all. The little girl heaved a sigh of relief.

"We need one more thing in our story," said Nathalie. "What can we add that will help us banish the ogre back to the Rocky Mountains and bring the seamstress home safe and sound to Frank?"

"Charlie!" all the children shouted at once. Miss Ryaness looked up sharply.

Nathalie put her fingers to her lips. "Shhh, we mustn't disturb the others. All right then, Charlie will leave the mine under Turtle Mountain. He'll go to the ogre's mountain and drag the ogre back inside."

"Charlie's not afraid of the dark, is he, Nathalie?" asked Delbert.

"Of course not," replied Nathalie. "Charlie's used to it." Charlie was one of the mine horses. He was a favourite of all the children, as he was the gentlest. Each year at the school picnic, Charlie was brought down from his stable at the mine entrance and the children took turns riding him. "So Charlie puts the ogre back in his place, then lets the seamstress get onto his back and he takes her all the way back to Frank where everyone is now safe from the Rocky Mountain Ogre. The end."

The children clapped. This time Miss Ryaness smiled; all the students were finished their work. Everyone, even the littlest, helped to tidy the schoolroom for the next day, then Miss Ryaness rang her handbell. School was over for the day.

CHAPTER 4
A Visit with Andy

THE SENIOR STUDENTS LINGERED IN THE schoolyard after the bell.

"Let's play Hull Gull," suggested Abby Hawe. Her dad managed the company accounts for the coal mine and he had passed on his love of numbers to his daughter. Abby loved to play any game that involved counting. She collected some pebbles from the schoolyard and distributed them to the others as they formed a circle. "Nathalie, you go first."

"Hull Gull, hands full, parcel, how many?" Nathalie thrust her clenched fist into the middle of the circle. Nathalie liked this game; it was one of the first she had learned at school.

"Two?" asked Lester, who was standing to her right. Nathalie opened her hand. There were four pebbles lying in her palm. "You have to give me two!" All the girls giggled.

"This is a stupid game," grumbled Lester, who wasn't very good at either guessing or doing sums. "Why do we have to play math games when school is over for the day? Let's swing Indian clubs." Swinging the weighted wooden clubs was a popular pastime for boys who wanted to develop strong arms, which was just about every one of them. The girls thought it rather unladylike.

"No fair!" cried the girls. "That's a boy's game. We'd rather play basketball."

"It's no fun to play basketball with girls!" said the boys. "You have too many rules."

"Well, then," announced Frances, "we're going to go see Andy. He's more interesting than any of you anyway!"

Albert Bansemer groaned. "Aw, he's just as stupid as that game. My dad says that his stories are all malarkey, and we shouldn't listen. My dad says we shouldn't sit around listening to those lies. My dad says we should play ball and run and stuff so we'll be strong enough to work in the mine next year. My dad says -"

"He's my dad too," broke in Frances, "and I've never heard him say any of that stuff. We're going to Andy's place. If you want to run around and swing clubs, go ahead." And with that, the five girls of the Senior class, noses high in the air, left the yard of the

Frank School. The moment they turned the corner they all burst into laughter.

"Boys!" Ruby Watkins, aged fourteen, gave a theatrical sigh. "Sometimes I wish they would all go down the mine and never come back!"

"That's for sure!" agreed Abby.

Nathalie looked at the two older girls in surprise. She would have given anything for a brother or a sister...or a father, for that matter. "You don't really mean that, do you, Ruby? They say it's awful down the mine."

Frances gave Nathalie a quick hug. "Of course Ruby doesn't mean it. She's just teasing."

"And boys are soooo easy to tease!" laughed Jessie Leitch, who was thirteen just like Frances and Nathalie. With a laugh, the five girls linked arms and walked in lockstep down Fifth Street to the bridge, on their way to what they called "the field side" of the creek. All five girls stopped on the bridge and leaned over to look into the water. They liked to see their reflections in the quiet pool on one side of the creek, just under the bridge.

"Hey, look!" cried Jessie. "We're on the bridge and we *are* a bridge!"

It was true. Ruby, who was the tallest, happened to be standing in the middle. On either side of her were Abby and Frances, both a little shorter, with round, smiling faces and big satin bows in their light hair.

Jessie, who was small and dark, was beside Abby, and Nathalie was at the end beside Frances. Reflected in the quiet pool, their heads made a perfect "∩" set atop the line of their linked arms, and together, they did mirror the shape of the wishing bridge.

"I'm always the shortest," complained Jessie. "I want to be tall!" Jessie stood on her tiptoes and ruined the line. Nathalie stood on her tiptoes too, then all the girls, laughing, did the same. But when they did, Ruby's head disappeared in the shadow of Turtle Mountain, which was also reflected in the water. All the girls instinctively moved away from the pool, and turned their backs on the mountain. The reflecting pool was the only quiet part of the creek; the rest of the water was gurgling cheerfully away from the mountain, away from the shadows.

"Time for our wish," announced Nathalie. Wishing from the bridge had become a tradition since the day she had spent underneath the old creaking timbers, and the idea had spread to her friends. They each threw a pebble into the water, closed their eyes, turned around once, and made a wish. In spite of the cheerful water, Nathalie sometimes had doubts about the ritual. She wondered where all the wishes went. They certainly were not coming true – not hers, at any rate. Did each wish cancel out the last? Were they all floating around somewhere until the one fine day they would be granted all at once? Or was it just nonsense?

Nathalie's mother didn't believe in wishing. She said that folks who made wishes were just asking to be disappointed. She said there was enough disappointment in this world already without asking for more. Nathalie knew that her mother had had many disappointments. Sometimes, and not just when Nathalie was dreaming, she thought that she was one of them.

Across the bridge the girls passed the miners' cottages on Alberta Avenue. There were seven of them, although one stood empty. The Bansemer house was the first in line, closest to the bridge and town, and Nathalie thought that it was the happiest place on earth. Mrs. Bansemer was always baking (she had to, she had so many children!) and could always be persuaded to make a bit of extra dough into a cinnamon whirligig for the girls to share. Today was no exception. Her mouth tingling with cinnamon, Nathalie skipped down the path with her friends.

When they reached the Watkins house, the girls formed a circle around Ruby so that she could not be seen. Quickly and quietly, they walked past. When they were out of earshot, they heaved a sigh of relief. Since Ruby's older brother Thomas had gone down the mine, Ruby's list of chores had grown enormously. Whenever they could help Ruby escape, they did. Of course, Ruby still had to do the chores, but it was sometimes easier if she had some free time with her friends first.

Past the cottages the girls started to run, just for the feel of the wind in their hair. They waved to Ellen and John Thornley at the shoe shop as they passed. Shortly after, Ruby and Abby, being one year older and therefore infinitely more refined, stopped their dash along the path and walked together, heads close, probably talking about the boys they had just left behind. Nathalie, Frances, and Jessie just kept on going.

A mile or so down the road the girls stopped and held their sides. "That felt good!" said Jessie. More slowly they continued to the edge of the Graham Ranch. That was where Andy Grissack Jr. lived. Andy was an old, gnarled trapper from Lethbridge. He hadn't had much schooling, but he could tell a fine story. The children of Frank loved his tales, even though the grown-ups sometimes accused him of exaggeration. He lived in a threadbare tent all year long and looked after himself just fine.

"Andy? You home?" called Frances. Andy's grizzled head poked out of the tent opening. "Why?" he replied with a grin. "Have I got some visitors?"

"No visitors," laughed Jessie. "Just us girls. Tell us a story, Andy. Please?"

Andy laughed and came outside. "So you want a story, do you? How about the Lost Lemon Mine? No, somehow today feels like a day for telling about the mountain. Our mountain, Turtle Mountain." Andy stopped and stared thoughtfully at the huge limestone mass that rose up behind them. "Yeah, today I've got a feeling that's the story I should tell." The girls settled onto chunks of log that were placed around Andy's fire and waited for the story to take them to another time and place.

CHAPTER 5
Napi and the Spirit Wife

"**N**OW YOU KNOW THAT ONCE THIS WAS ALL water, don't you?" The girls looked at one another. That wasn't what Miss Ryaness had taught them in class. Andy caught the look. "Gals," he sighed. "I told you before. What's in your history books and what's in your storybooks is different stuff. What's in the history books tells what really happened, or leastaways what the folks who write the books think really happened. What's in the storybooks helps a person make sense of the world. Whether it's true or not don't matter, it's how it makes you think that counts. And the Blackfoot people who tell this story, they be real good thinkers. So forget your history for a while and start thinking like them." He took a deep breath.

"So everything was water, there was no earth, only the sky up yonder and the water all down here. The Spirits, now they lived in the Sky, and the Swimmers lived in the Water. But there weren't no Walkers, like you and me.

"So one day the wife of the Great Spirit who was in charge of stuff up in that Skyland there, she looks down from the sky and sees something glitter. That's not a Swimmer, she's thinking. So what is it? This Spirit Wife leans way far over the edge of the Sky to see the glittery thing better, and she leans too far over and she falls right out of the Sky. Worst of all," and at this point Andy's voice gets quiet and the girls know they are about to hear mention of an unmentionable, so they lean in close, "worst of all, this Spirit Wife's going to have a baby real soon. And here she is, falling right out of the sky!" Andy just shook his head at such behaviour.

"So the Spirit Wife's falling, and all the time she's wishing that somebody would catch her and put her down someplace safe where she can have this baby. But you and me know she's going to have to wish real hard, because there's no place to put her, as things stand in the story up to now. All I can say, it's a good thing she's a Spirit person, 'cause if she were an ordinary person she'd really be out of luck. I don't know about you, but I haven't had much luck with wishing, myself personal."

Nathalie looked hard at Andy. Did he believe in wishes? She wondered what Andy had wished, and if he had been disappointed, like her mother.

"Now the Spirit Wife's falling, falling, falling. And the Swans who are part of the whole great nation of Swimmers look up and they see her coming. And they say to each other, well look here, there's a great galumph of a woman falling out of the sky. And they know she's not a Swimmer so they fly up in the air and they grab her hair in their beaks and they stop her from falling."

Andy suddenly grabbed his own long, greasy, grey hair with his two hands and pretended to be the Spirit Wife, jerked right out of the air by two swans. His head bobbed, his eyes popped, and his tongue lolled out of his mouth. The girls laughed, even Ruby and Abby, who had quietly joined the group as the story was unravelling.

"Course, now the Swans have got a problem. Where to put her? She has these two long legs but there isn't any earth for her to be standing on. But see, the Swimmers know a secret. They know that deep under all that water there's earth. So they holler out to all the other Swimmers and they say, you folks go on down there and bring some of that earth up here so we can put this great galumph down. And then they say, you got to hurry, too, cause it looks like she's having a baby. So the Swimmers, they all take turns, but none of them can go deep enough to get the earth. And they all come back, gasping like drowned fish, all tired out.

"Finally Muskrat tries. Muskrat is one of the strongest Swimmers. He dives deep, deeper than any of the others. But it isn't deep enough. So he goes deeper. Still nothing, and now it's real dark, because he's too far away from the surface and everything's all black and cold. Still nothing. Finally, Muskrat he knows he's a goner if he don't get back topside. His lungs are right ready to bust. Last thing he does before he starts to swim back up is take a final swipe at the bottom. He's getting mad, you see, all that effort for nothing. And you know, he touches it. He's there! He gets a wee little bit of earth in his paw and off he goes back to the top.

"When Muskrat gets back, though, the other Swimmers think he couldn't do it, like all the rest, and Muskrat, he's too tired to say. So he just holds up his paw and there's the earth. But it's hardly any, not enough for the Spirit Wife to stand on. So now what? Turtle, slow Turtle, now she gets a chance to be in the story. She swims real slow, real close, and she says, 'Put the earth on my back. She can stand on me.' So that's just what Muskrat does, he puts the earth on Turtle's back. An' if you look, you can still see Muskrat's paw-print on Turtle's shell."

Nathalie smiled inside. Andy knew so many things! Next time she saw a turtle, she was going to look to see Muskrat's pawprint. Nathalie was one of Miss Ryaness's best students, and she knew perfectly well that animal markings had a great deal more to do with camouflage than with Sky Spirits, but she didn't care. As Andy said, this was a story. And one never knew when one might come upon a place where the story world and the real world touched. Just maybe it was on Turtle's back.

"Now the Swans are getting tired of holding the Spirit Wife up by her hair, and they're real happy about Turtle's offer. They let her down, real gentle, on the earth on Turtle's back. And so the Spirit Wife, she gets her wish, see, because she's got a safe place to have her baby. So now we got the Sky, and we got the Earth, and we got the Water, and they're all together and that makes magic happen. That itty bit of earth, it starts to grow, just like when the Grahams spill all their manure over the field and it spreads out like a great smelly puddle. And it spreads and spreads, and now the Spirit Wife has got lots of room, so she goes right ahead and has that baby of hers. And when that job is done, don't the Swans just grab her by the hair and fly her back to her home in the sky."

"But what about the baby?" asked Frances, who was very used to babies. "Didn't his mother take him back to the sky?"

"Now there's a thing," replied Andy thoughtfully. "I guess them Spirit folks don't behave like us Walking folks. She leaves her baby right there on Turtle's back. Of course, not before she gives him a name; she calls him Napi. And Napi, he don't behave like us folks either. He gets right up on his two long legs, even though he's just been borned, and he sets to walking all over the earth that's spread out all around him. And everyplace he walks, he makes new creatures, all o' them walking around on legs – two legs, four legs, six legs, whatever."

"Six legs!" the girls burst out laughing. "Well, you never know," replied Andy with a grin.

"Anyway, he makes up all the creatures with not too many mistakes, and then he goes back to Turtle, where he was borned. And you know, that earth on Turtle's back, it up and swallowed him whole." The girls gasped.

"Yup, this here is Turtle Mountain, this one we're looking at 'cross the river from this old tent. Chief Running Wolf, who lives hereabouts, he told me this is the place where Napi lives. Well now, I don't know about that, cause do you think a Spirit person like Napi would sit still for all those miners cutting holes in his house? It doesn't make any sense to me. If I was Napi, I'd be right cross about all the noise. And maybe he is, too. Sometimes this old mountain shakes like crazy. You and me, well we think it's the miners doing their blasting and such, but that's not what Chief Running Wolf's people think. They used to say that the shaking came from Turtle, who needed a stretch. That's why they call Turtle Mountain 'the mountain that walks.' I guess it must be hard work, holding the whole earth on your back all the time. But lately, they've been saying something different."

Andy got very quiet, which was rare for Andy. "What do they say?" Jessie prompted.

"They say the shaking isn't coming from Turtle. It's Napi. Napi's angry, and Chief Running Wolf's people say that's a real bad thing."

CHAPTER 6
Lights

AFTER VISITING WITH ANDY, THE GIRLS wandered back along the path towards town. The story had left them uneasy; it was so different from all of Andy's other tales. Usually they laughed a lot, and there was always a happy ending. Perhaps the feeling came from the fact that it was getting dark, and Turtle Mountain was shrouded in shadows. Surely no angry god or ogre lived inside; it was just as Andy had said, the stories weren't real, they just made a person think. But what if the stories *were* real? The Blackfoot people had lived in the area for centuries, and like Andy said, they were good thinkers. They didn't tell stories just for fun; their stories had important meanings. Nathalie glanced over her shoulder at Turtle Mountain. She shivered. "The mountain is just a big rock," she told herself. "There's no Spirit inside." But now that she had heard Napi's story, Nathalie wasn't convinced. More than ever, she was glad that she wasn't a miner.

As the girls passed the shoe shop, they saw the Thornleys locking the door. "Hello again!" called out Ellen.

"Miss Thornley, I heard that you will be taking the train to your home tomorrow. It was very nice to have you visit Frank," said Frances politely.

"That's a nice thing to say," replied Ellen, "and I thank you. I've had a wonderful visit with my brother, but it's time to go home. And guess what? John is treating me to the hotel in town for my last night! My train doesn't leave until dinnertime tomorrow, so there's no reason why we can't stay here at the shop and walk over tomorrow, but no, John says to me, let's stay in town for your last night and have a nice dinner. Isn't he just the finest of brothers?"

"Yes, Miss Thornley. Have a good trip," called the girls as they passed. When they were well ahead, Jessie, Frances, Ruby, and Abby all exchanged glances. They couldn't imagine their brothers treating them with anything less than total disdain, and a dinner and night at the hotel were beyond imagining. Nathalie lowered her eyes. Once again, she felt left out. She was sure that if she had a brother, or a sister, they would be the best of friends.

They came to Ruby's house first, and as expected, her mother was waiting on the porch holding a broom. Next they passed the Ennis cottage, then the Ackroyd cottage. That was where Lester lived with his mom and stepdad. Nathalie kept her eyes down, but tried to look sideways to see if Lester was there.

Next they dropped off Jessie. Little Allen Roy, Jessie's eight-year-old brother, was holding baby Marion in his arms. "Mom says you're to change her and feed her," he said, handing the wet bundle over. "I'm to help with the firewood."

As Jessie adjusted Marion on her hip, Nathalie tickled the little girl under her chin. Marion laughed. "Nattie, Nattie!" she laughed, trying to pull on Nathalie's braids.

The girls continued on to the Bansemer cabin. As always, the gas lamps were already lit and laughter drifted out of the windows. Frances hugged Nathalie goodbye. "See you tomorrow!"

Abby and Nathalie, the only two who lived on the town side of Gold Creek, continued across the bridge. The reflecting pool was riled, and they couldn't see themselves. They threw their wish pebbles into the water anyway, and went on into Frank proper. At the corner of Dominion Avenue, Abby continued straight ahead along Fifth Street – she lived one block over on King Street with all her brothers and sisters. Even though there were lots in her family, Abby always seemed to have new hair ribbons. Nathalie didn't mind about the ribbons; she did envy her the brothers and sisters.

Nathalie turned left down Dominion towards the mountain. She and her mother shared a small white house just one wooden sidewalk off Dominion. Nathalie carefully kept her eyes lowered to the ground until she was almost to her front door. Today's wish had been for lights in the window. Lights would mean that her mother wasn't working late, that her mother was at home cooking dinner and waiting for Nathalie to come home. Lights would mean that Nathalie wouldn't have to make her own dinner and go to bed by herself. Lights would mean that her mother wouldn't be too tired to talk a little. Lights would be good.

Nathalie waited until the last possible moment, and then looked up.

Lights!

CHAPTER 7
A Letter from Aunt Sadie

S HE RACED INSIDE AND FLEW INTO THE kitchen. "Mama, how was your day?" she cried, and she gave her mother a tight hug.

"It was busy," replied her mother. "But I'm home now, and that makes it a good day." Dinner was ready, and the two sat down at their tiny table and talked about their days. Nathalie told her mother about Lester, and how he never seemed to want to play with her anymore, even though they had been best friends when they were younger. She told her about Mrs. Bansemer's whirligigs, and Ellen Thornley's night at the hotel. She told of the story she had made up about the ogre, and Andy's story about Napi, and how the tales had disturbed her. Somehow, after she was finished with all the telling, Nathalie felt less uneasy.

After dinner, Nathalie collected their dishes and put on the kettle for some tea. As she bustled happily about the kitchen, her mother sat quietly, watching her. Her daughter was growing up so fast. And growing up well: Nathalie had a quiet determination to make the best of life. Where that came from, her mother could only imagine. Shaking her head slightly, she smiled at her daughter's back.

Nathalie brought her mother a cup of tea. "My turn," said her mother. "I have a surprise for you. Do you remember your cousin Helena, from Spokane?"

Nathalie remembered a photograph of a beautiful little girl with long blonde curls in a dark green velvet dress with real lace. She had never met her cousin, as Helena and her mother lived with Grandfather. Helena had been beautiful, like a porcelain doll. "I remember," replied Nathalie.

"Well, your Aunt Sadie wrote to me. Helena is an only child, just like you, and we thought it might be nice, just for a while, if Helena was to come and visit with us. She could go to school with you, and meet your friends. Would you like that?"

Like that? Nathalie felt like Victoria Day fireworks were exploding in her heart. It would be like having a sister! But Nathalie knew it was too good to be true.

"What about Grandfather?" she asked quietly. Her mother looked down into her lap. "It seems that Grandfather has business to look after in New York.

He will be away for a goodly amount of time. Sadie thought it would be a fine opportunity for her to make a visit to Frank."

Nathalie felt the familiar pain behind her eyes. Grandfather didn't know that Aunt Sadie and Helena were coming. After all this time, he was still disappointed in them. But the hurt was an old one and she pushed it back, as she always did, and thought of the visit. Her excitement came back in a rush and she jumped up and squeezed her mother nearly in half.

"Enough!" laughed her mother. "I'm glad you're happy, because she is coming tonight."

"Tonight? How?" Mother had just received the letter today. Aunt Sadie and Helena were coming in via Lethbridge on the Spokane Flyer, the brand-new passenger railway service. Mother explained that she had checked with the station master, and he had told her that the train would be delayed because of a late spring snowstorm.

"Mr. Baker, down at the station, has promised to send a messenger to me when he knows the time of arrival. But it will be very late, or early actually, tomorrow morning. So, hard as it is, we both must go to sleep. I promise I will wake you when it's time, but bed first."

The two of them finished their tea and washed up their few dishes, making plans all the time for their guests. Nathalie tried to imagine what Helena would look like now. Would she still have curls? It was the fashion for young ladies to wear their hair very long, curled into ringlets and tied with a great satin ribbon. Nathalie fingered her braids. As a baby, she'd had curly hair, but when she was four, Nathalie had come down with a terrible case of the measles. It was a deadly disease. In fact, her father had caught measles from her and the disease had killed him. Nathalie had survived, but her hair, from that time forward, had been perfectly straight. Mostly, Nathalie just wanted her hair out of her way, but tonight was special.

"Mama, would you curl my hair?" she pleaded when their chores were done. Her mother hesitated a moment, a flash of the day's fatigue in her eyes, but she went to the bedroom and got their comb and the rags they used to tie Nathalie's straight hair into ringlets. Nathalie held their small hand mirror as her mother undid the braids and began to comb her hair. She watched as her mother separated a lock of hair and tied a clean rag in a knot over the end of it, then deftly wound the hair into a tight roll, tying another knot round the lock to hold it close to Nathalie's head. While her mother worked, Nathalie tried to imagine what cousin Helena might look like.

Her mother's thoughts were not on Helena, but on Nathalie. The face she saw reflected in the tiny mirror was so different from her own. Mother and daughter might dress the same, with their white blouses, dark skirts, practical black stockings, and button-up boots, but there the resemblance ended. Nathalie's mother saw the face of her beloved husband, softened in Nathalie, and felt her love for them both welling up. The striking dark colouring and lovely thick hair signified to her the great depths in their personalities, depths yet to be explored in Nathalie. Her clear, dark eyes were so full of promise, but far too serious for a girl her age.

That's my fault, thought the woman known as Mrs. Vaughan. I did that to her. She is smart and lovely and generous and loyal, but I have buried her in my painful memories, memories that have left me a pale shell of the person I could have become. I should be a daughter, a wife, a woman named Caroline, but all I am is Mrs. Vaughan, barely able to even feed my daughter, who is the only good and beautiful part of my life. But I know she loves me. How can that be?

Nathalie caught her mother looking at her reflection in the mirror. She made a funny face, made sillier still by the rags sticking out in all directions from her head. Her mother's eyes crinkled at the corners, and she couldn't help but smile. Then she quickly looked away, so that her perceptive daughter would not catch a glimpse of the tears in her eyes.

And for the time that was left before bed, Nathalie sat at her mother's feet, feeling her mother's hands on her head, listening to her tell stories of her childhood with Sadie. The fire in the cookstove died down to embers as Caroline told of exploring the meadows with her sister and of baking ginger cookies with the loving grandmother who had died before Nathalie's birth. Caroline told of a time when Grandfather's parlour had been full of light and the portraits had seemed to smile; stories filled with sunshine and laughter.

So this is what it feels like to have wishes come true, Nathalie thought.

CHAPTER 8
The Night Crew

OUTSIDE, THE TEMPERATURE WAS DROPPING. As the evening turned into night, an icy haze hovered over the top of Turtle Mountain, which loomed dark under the moonlight. William Warrington looked up at it as he left his sleeping family in their makeshift cabin on the field side of Gold Creek, reminding himself, as he did every night, that it was time to find them a larger place in town. He shivered as he made his way across the wooden bridge. His job with the Canadian-American Coal and Coke Company was a good one: the mining was easier than in most places, the town was a reasonably civilized place to raise children, and the money was good.

But there was something about Turtle Mountain that didn't seem quite right. Maybe it was the fact that its immense height, 7,236 feet, blocked out the sun after three o'clock every summer afternoon. Maybe it was the odd rumblings and creaking that could be heard almost constantly throughout the mine. Maybe it was old Andy's stories about the Blackfoot legend...yes, that must be it! Warrington laughed at himself. He was just letting Andy's tales get the better of his imagination, that's all. A mountain was just a mountain, a mine was just a job. No more, no less.

John Watkins, Ruby's father, and Alex Clark, Albert's father, joined William Warrington. They were the only three of the night crew that lived on the far side of the creek. They walked companionably together onto Dominion Street, passing the Imperial Hotel, where the bar was beginning to fill with miners from the early shift, who were all finished with work for the day. They passed Leitch's furniture store and Warrington eyed a chair that he intended to buy for his wife when they finally moved to town.

On the wooden sidewalk outside of the Palm Restaurant, they met up with some of the other men of the night crew: Alex Tashigan, who worked at the mine tipple, Halfpint Jones, Shorty Dawson, Dan McKenzie, Alex McPhail, Alex Grant, talkative Charlie Farrell, and Fred Farrington. All the men were dressed alike in dirty coveralls, wool jackets with brass buttons, heavy leather boots, and dark blue sailor's pea caps. Each carried a tin bucket filled with his lunch.

The group walked on down the length of Dominion Avenue where Joseph Chapman, an experienced miner from Wales and foreman of the night crew, was waiting impatiently at the mining office for the sixteen miners to arrive. The night crew's duties involved checking the work of the day crew, replacing damaged timbers, and inspecting equipment for the next day's extraction of coal. They all knew their jobs well, and as a group, the men headed towards the mine entrance that lay just past the end of Dominion Avenue.

"What kind of weather is this we're having?" asked Farrell. "April's been nice and warm till now, but we're like as not to freeze our long underwear tonight."

"Look at the ice haze over the mountain," replied Warrington, pointing out the phenomenon he had noted earlier. "I won't be surprised if we get snow."

It had just gone midnight when the men reached the mine entrance. The mine horses were stabled at the entrance, and some of the men spent a few minutes giving them food and water. Warrington took "Charlie," the children's favourite, and put the specially designed hard hat over his ears and strapped it under the bridle. The men joked that the horses had been given hard hats before the miners themselves.

Warrington needed Charlie that night to help him pull some of the heavy timbers they used for braces. The braces were squared logs, two foot by two foot and as tall as the tunnels in the mine, and they were wrestled into place when tunnels were built, to help brace the ceiling. The timbers were huge, and heavy. They could withstand enormous stresses. But lately, strange things had been happening inside the mine. Timbers placed brand new by the night crew would be found splintered by the day crew. Coal extracted and left stored in cracks and fissures one day would disappear by the next, the fissure closed, as if the mountain had swallowed it up. Warrington, as timber chief, knew that at least some of the timbers, for reasons inexplicable to him, would need replacing that night, and for that job he needed Charlie.

The sedimentary rock inside of Turtle Mountain was riddled with tunnels. It was a mountain that nearly mined itself, some of the advertisements had said. The coal, said to be among the best in Canada, was in easy-to-reach seams throughout the mountain. Little blasting was required to reach it, which cut down greatly on expenses. And because the coal seams were nearly straight up and down, coal could be mined at the top of the mountain and merely rolled down the chute to the main tunnel far below.

In most mines, the coal was found deep underground. It had to be blasted out, and then lifted to the surface, which required a great deal more manpower. In Frank, a huge amount of high quality coal, nearly 1,000 tons every day, had been taken with little trouble from inside the successful Frank Mine every day since the mine's opening two years earlier.

Alex Tashigan turned at the entrance to make his way to the weigh scale at the mine tipple. The tipple was the building where the waste rock was separated from the coal, so that the coal could then be weighed and loaded onto railway cars. As Tashigan went off, Alex Clark called out an invitation to meet for lunch at the mine entrance at four in the morning. Tashigan waved his acceptance.

Joseph Chapman led the way into the mine. The entrance was as tall as three men and framed by the huge timbers. Train tracks ran down the center. The miners walked into the mountain on either side of the tracks, skirting the coal cars that brought the coal to the tipple for weighing. As they lit the small lamps attached to their hard hats, some of the gloom of the tunnel was dispelled, but it was still a grim place. The atmosphere was ominous. There was a sense that bad things could happen to those who entered. But if the miners noticed, they did not say.

The miners followed Chapman, with groups of two and three breaking off to take different tunnels. Each group knew exactly what they had to do and needed little supervision. They were professionals. William Warrington, leading Charlie, brought up the rear. He could hear the men ahead of him exclaiming about the amount of rock littering the tunnel floors.

It was if the mountain had shaken itself like a dog, scattering chunks of coal everywhere. And it must have shaken since the day crew had gone home, or they would have picked it all up and prepared it to be loaded onto the night train that transported the coal out of Frank. No wonder Turtle Mountain was a money-maker. It really did mine itself, thought Warrington.

He led Charlie, as docile a horse as ever lived, into the dark mine. He chose a tunnel that had been giving him trouble for days. Even though he knew better, Warrington could almost imagine that the tunnel was alive. Every day he and Charlie replaced the timbers holding up the roof. Every day the tunnel squeezed and squeezed until it crushed and splintered the new timbers. As often as he replaced those timbers, Warrington knew that when he returned he would have to replace them again. And tonight the sight in the tunnel was just as he had expected. He sighed, and he and Charlie got to work.

CHAPTER 9
The Trainmen

J
UST OUTSIDE OF FRANK, AN OLD FREIGHT TRAIN chugged its way slowly into town. It was a steep climb into Frank, not easy on the locomotive. The engineer, a man by the name of Ben Murgatroyd, was at the throttle, looking intently into the darkness for any trouble on the tracks. Behind him the fireman, Bud Lahey, stoked the boiler for more power. Several cars back, in the caboose, Train Conductor Henri Pettit checked the time. They were late. The snowstorm that had held up the Spokane Flyer had slowed all train traffic.

The brakemen, Sid Choquette and Bill Lowes, had fallen half asleep as they waited to arrive in Frank. As Chief Engineer Murgatroyd finally eased the labouring locomotive into the station, the conductor jumped down to confer with the local agent. The station wasn't much of a place, only a spare boxcar, but at least it was warm. The conductor and the agent sat down near the pot-bellied stove in the boxcar and studied the schedules.

Pettit sighed. It appeared that his freight train would have to lay over on a rail siding until the Spokane Flyer passed them at about 4:30 a.m. The layover would put them even further behind schedule, but there was nothing for it except to wait. He had Murgatroyd ease the train onto the siding, then Pettit sent the locomotive up to the mine to pick up the coal cars that had been filled to the brim by the miners working the day shift. At least, thought Pettit, they could bring the full cars down to the siding and hook them up to the rest of the train while they waited for the Flyer. That way, when the track was finally theirs, they would be right ready to go. So while his men chugged up to the mine tipple, Conductor Pettit put his feet up by the pot-bellied stove and prepared for a long and annoying wait.

Murgatroyd had some fancy negotiating to do on the small spur line that led to the mine. First he backed up to the two full coal cars at the mine tipple. The two brakemen, Choquette and Lowes, scrambled about in the cold darkness to hook the cars to the locomotive. Then Murgatroyd made his way down to the siding and used another spur line to hook the cars to the main part of the train. Then Choquette and Lowes hooked an empty coal car to the locomotive. Back up to the mine tipple they went. Choquette and Lowes unhooked the empty car for the miners to fill the next day. Choquette carefully set the brakes on the empty car. The job was done. All they had to do was take the locomotive back to the siding, hook it back up to the train, and wait for the Flyer.

As Murgatroyd slowly eased the locomotive down the rail spur, Choquette and Lowes stopped for a minute to chat with Alex Tashigan, who had come down from the weigh scale, and Alex Clark and Fred Farrington, who had arrived to eat their lunch. It was 4 a.m. The men shared a couple of jokes, then were startled by a slight tremor under their feet.

"Ah, Turtle Mountain walks again!" laughed Clark. All the men laughed with him. They had heard the stories told not only by Andy Grissack but also by most of the Native people who lived in those parts. Not a one of the miners believed that Napi lived inside the mountain on the back of a turtle that walked. These men knew that the tremors were simply caused by the earth settling around the tunnels in the mine. They knew that the tunnels were dug in places that would not place undue stress on the mountain. The miners knew the difference between stories and reality.

The men chatted a bit longer as they looked down at the town of Frank stretched out below them. As they saw messengers begin to make their way from the train station to wake up the train travellers at the hotel, Choquette and Lowes said their goodbyes and walked down the spur line to catch up with the slowly moving locomotive.

It was quiet at that late hour. As he ate, Alex Clark looked off to the west where his cabin lay, his sleeping family safe inside. It always gave him a warm feeling to look down on them at night. He felt proud that his safety work in the mine gave them the security of a good life. Little did he know that on that particular night his eldest daughter Lillian was not at home, but staying in town. She worked at the Imperial Hotel. That night, with so many travelers laying over to wait for the delayed Spokane Flyer, she had had to work so late that her mother had given her permission for the first time in her life to stay in town at the hotel until morning. But at 4 a.m., Lillian was finally asleep in her borrowed bed.

Nathalie's mother was asleep as well. So was Frances Bansemer in the big bed she shared with her sisters. So was Lester Johnson in the cabin two doors down from the Bansemers. So was Andy Grissack in his threadbare tent. Nathalie was not. She was at her bedroom window, looking at the ice haze over Turtle Mountain, listening for the Spokane Flyer.

It was 4:08 a.m.

CHAPTER 10
Turtle Walks

A T FIRST NATHALIE THOUGHT THAT IT WAS starting to hail. The roof over her head was reverberating with tiny pings, sounds that were getting more frequent every second. Then she heard a jarring crack of thunder, louder and closer than anything she had ever heard before. "Mama?" she called. The entire house began to shake.

"Mama!" There was a tremendous whoosh of air and the windowpane in front of her shattered.

AT THE MINE TIPPLE, Tashigan, Clark, and Farrington felt the earth shaking beneath them. "My God, man!" shouted Farrington in horror, as the three men leapt to their feet.

The top of Turtle Mountain was shattering. It felt

like some great ogre was rearing up within the mountain and breaking through the top, hurling monstrous chunks of limestone angrily down into the valley. The three men strained their eyes, looking in confusion through the darkness above, as nearly ninety million tons of limestone broke away from the mountain and careened down the slope straight towards them.

ANDY GRISSACK WAS PULLED from a deep sleep. He didn't know if he had heard or felt the strange deep roar. He crawled out of his tent. He looked up and became rigid with terror. He thought of Napi.

MURGATROYD FELT THE SHIVER in the ground. Then he heard the horrendous crack. Instinctively, he yelled a warning to Choquette and Lowes. He pushed the throttle hard, forcing the old locomotive to leap forward. The two brakemen ran, leaping for the handrails at the back of the locomotive to haul themselves up. The train surged ahead. The men turned back to look. They saw the slide toss the three miners at the tipple high into the air. They saw the slide swallow them. Then they held on for dear life as Murgatroyd raced the train across the eastern bridge that spanned the creek. Behind them, the colossal boulders crashed into the bridge, hurling it sideways and throwing it into the water below.

INSIDE THE MINE, Charlie lurched. He hit the wall of the tunnel. William Warrington staggered. The mine was beginning to move, rolling from side to side. Warrington felt as if he were standing on the deck of a ship, rolling with the waves. He saw cracks form all around him. Coal rained down on his head.

"Get out! Get out! The tunnels are collapsing!" Warrington heard the foreman's frantic shouts echo through the mine just as one of the braces beside him splintered and broke. The top half fell free, knocking Warrington down and fracturing his thigh. With his body pinned under the brace, he could only twist his face to the side to try and protect it from the coal that continued to shower him. His lamp went out. The shouts of the other miners grew faint and then disappeared as sections of tunnels collapsed around him.

OUTSIDE, the mine entrance disappeared. The power plant was crushed. The empty rail car that Choquette and Lowes had just parked at the tipple was thrown high into the air, landing two miles away. The boulders continued to boil angrily down the mountainside, pushing a powerful wall of frigid air in front of them. That invisible wall rushed into the valley, tearing apart everything in its path. Trees were ripped out by their roots, houses torn from their foundations. Behind the wall of air, the rocks followed, burying everything that was left.

The slide rampaged on, crossing the railway line and ploughing into the miners' temporary cabins. William Warrington's house disappeared. The Graham Ranch was buried. Andy Grissack was swept away. Still the slide raced on. It crushed the Thornleys' shoe shop. It kept on going till it reached the row of houses on Alberta Avenue at the bottom of the valley.

The rocks were plunging so fast that they were hot, so fast that they could not stop when they reached the bottom. The force of the slide propelled the boulders halfway up the far side of the next mountain. An impenetrable cloud of limestone dust blanketed the entire valley. Almost everything on the field side of Gold Creek was just...gone.

Finally, there was silence. Turtle Mountain settled back, missing its top and suffering a grotesque gash all down its side. Debris was piled up around its feet, where fires were beginning to smoulder. There was no movement anywhere, except for the growing flames.

IT WAS 4:10 A.M. The slide had lasted just ninety seconds.

CHAPTER 11
A Cloud of Confusion

N ATHALIE FELT HER MOTHER SHAKING HER shoulder. "Nattie, Nattie, wake up! Are you all right?"

Nathalie felt dazed, and her head hurt. It was cold. She reached up to touch her forehead and her fingers came away wet. It was too dark to see, but she thought it was blood. Blood? Her mother helped her to sit on the bed, but Nathalie was still disoriented. She was sure that the bed used to be on the other side of the room. Nathalie felt her mother's hands leave her shoulders; a few moments later Nathalie could see the soft glow of their lamp. The bed *was* on the other side of the room! And she really was bleeding. And the window was broken; that was why it was cold.

"Mama, what happened? Was it a storm? I thought I heard thunder."

"I don't know," replied her mother. "I just don't know. I can't see anything outside. You're bleeding! Let me see your head."

As her mother bandaged the cut on her forehead, Nathalie tried to peer out the window. It looked like they were in a cloud. She remembered a terrible noise, and then the window had exploded in her face.

"Your cut isn't too serious," said her mother, with a sigh of relief. "You wait here. I'm going out to find out what happened." In moments, her mother had dressed and was gone, leaving Nathalie alone. She went back to the window. It truly was impossible to see anything, but sounds were beginning to filter through. There was shouting, a lot of shouting, and crying too. Nathalie felt a kind of fear that she had never felt before. Something really bad had happened. Really, really bad. Something that would change everything.

Nathalie got dressed, so she could be ready. For what, she didn't know. Now what should she do? Where was her mother? What was happening? Had something bad happened to her mother? Nathalie felt paralyzed. She sat on the edge of the bed with her hands under her legs, shivering. Every part of her body was held tight, and she barely breathed. Her back started to ache with the tension.

Finally her mother came back. She was coughing, and her face was completely white, but whether that was from horror or the white cloud outside, Nathalie couldn't tell.

"Mother?" Her voice came out in a whisper. Her mother waved Nathalie away as she rushed for a glass of water to clear her throat.

"It's Turtle Mountain. It broke apart, and caused a terrible landslide. There doesn't seem to be much damage, thank goodness. There's one big boulder in the center of town, but otherwise Frank seems to be intact. People are frightened, though. And, of course, we don't yet know how much damage there might be outside of town."

"What do you mean, Mama, 'outside of town'? Do you mean Blairmore? Did the slide hit the town of Blairmore?" Blairmore was only two miles away.

Nathalie's mother lowered her eyes. "No, the slide hit much closer than that."

"How close? Where did it hit? Where, Mama?" Nathalie could feel panic welling up inside her belly. She could guess what her mother wasn't saying. Nathalie had always known when her mother was trying to protect her; she had been able to tell since she was three years old. Why wouldn't her mother just tell her, and let her cry? Why did she have to pretend? She could feel that pressure behind her eyes coming back, that pain that came when she tried to keep tears inside, when she tried to bury the things that hurt.

"Mama, I'm not a child. Tell me!"

"Nathalie, they don't really know anything for sure, there's no point —"

"Tell me!"

"They're worried about the people on the other side of Gold Creek. What do you girls call it? The field side. They think...they think maybe it's buried."

Buried.

Frances, Jessie, and Ruby. Lester. Little Billy Warrington and his gopher tails. Baby Marion. Could they really all be buried?

Nathalie was very still. Her mother had her hand to her mouth, as if she was wishing that she could have stopped the words before they flew out into the air to hurt her daughter. But Nathalie wasn't hurt, not yet. She was thinking. They didn't know for sure, did they? If the field side was buried, then that was clearly the worst that could happen. If you started with that possibility, then any news had to be better. The men would dig people out; some would be rescued. The slide could be smaller than they thought. Some houses might have been spared. Nathalie decided that she would try to accept the possibility that they were all gone. And then she could be happy about every person that they found.

And she would help find them.

Nathalie stood up suddenly. Now she had something to do. She marched herself to the door and began pulling on her boots. "Mama, thank you. Now I know the worst. But it might not be that bad. We have to go help. We have to find my friends. And if we find even one, we'll feel better than we feel right now, won't we?"

Nathalie's mother sank down on the bed and stared at her daughter in surprise. Then she smiled, a tiny, crooked smile that Nathalie had never seen before. "Can you be that brave?"

Nathalie nodded her head yes, but there were tears rolling down her cheeks.

Her mother slumped and bowed her head. "I think you're right, Nattie, you *can* be that brave. I just don't know if I can. I came to Frank with such high hopes, but they died with your father. And now this. I don't know if I have any courage left." To Nathalie's amazement, her mother began to cry.

She ran to her mother and hugged her tight. "We can do it together, Mama," she whispered. Nathalie felt her mother's arms go around her and hold her close. And even though the sense of panic still resided in her belly, the pressure behind her eyes disappeared.

CHAPTER 12
Chaos

NATHALIE'S MOTHER FOUND TWO CLEAN cloths from their ragbag and dampened them from the pitcher. She wrapped one around her mouth and nose and helped Nathalie do the same. Then they ventured out into the cloud.

Once outside, Nathalie watched her mother hesitate, then pull herself up tall. It was as if she were wrapping a coat of determination around her. Nathalie tried to stand tall too. A man rushed by them. "Is that you, Mrs. Vaughan?" he called. "Please, can you go to the Imperial? It's chaos over there. They need someone with a clear head to take charge. Hurry!"

Nathalie's mother grabbed her hand and with a purposeful stride marched them both in the direction – or what they thought was the direction – of the hotel.

They were needed. Maybe her grandfather didn't need them, but Frank did. It was enough. Nathalie matched her mother stride for stride.

The hotel lobby was filled with people, and the many lamps that had been brought in made the place glow just like Christmas. Groups of men were congregating to compare notes. Some were sure that it was an explosion inside the mine. Explosions were, unfortunately, a very common occurrence in coal mines because of the noxious gases that tended to build up in the tunnels.

Others said no, it was an earthquake. Some thought it was a freak storm. Did you hear that wind? they asked one another. There was only one thing for sure. There were fires burning on the field side of Gold Creek. That's where help was needed.

Nathalie's mother was whisked away by the proprietor of the hotel the instant she walked in the door. "Take charge of the kitchen. We need hot food, soup, and coffee, and maybe sandwiches. Lots of them!" he ordered. As she was pulled away, she looked over her shoulder at Nathalie. "Stay close," she called. "And be careful!"

Nathalie looked around. The men were forming groups and leaving the hotel to head toward Gold Creek. There were a few women, most still in their nightclothes, some crying, some standing about talking quietly. Nathalie went to the door. "Old Bill," a local character, came wandering by. "'Scuse, lassie," he murmured. "Had a bit too much of the demon rum tonight, that's certain. The whole world's a-shaking...."

He wandered off. Nathalie shook her head, and tried to peer through the gloom. She could see bodies rushing in all directions, but no one seemed to be in charge. What did they need? What could she do? She could just barely see the glow of the fires on the other side of the creek. They looked ghostly through the limestone dust. Fire was always a danger, since the town was completely built of wood. That was it! She could collect buckets for the men to use to put out the fires! Nathalie rushed back into the hotel and found the proprietor.

"Good thinking, girl," he replied when she made her request. "Our buckets are in the back shed."

Nathalie raced outside. She collected as many buckets as she could find and ran towards the creek. "Whoa, there!" shouted a tall figure, the bank manager Nathalie guessed. "I'll take those. You can't be going over the creek. Not a slip of a girl like you. Home to your mama, now."

Nathalie handed over the buckets. Now what? It was tempting in the darkness to sneak over the creek and see the damage. She could do it in a minute. But Nathalie was not quite ready to see. And she knew she couldn't help over there. Just then, a tiny girl sidled up beside her. "I want my mama!" she cried.

Nathalie reached down and took the little girl's hand. The poor thing was freezing. She thought it might be the girl who had worn the blue pinny to school that day, the one who was afraid of the ogre, but the girl was covered in too much dust to tell. "Let's get you warm," said Nathalie, and turned to go back to the hotel.

By the time she reached the lobby, she had made several false turns, and collected three more wandering children. The dust cloud made it impossible to tell direction. Nathalie was grateful when she finally saw the glowing lamps of the hotel through the dark. As she walked into the lobby, she could tell the atmosphere had changed. The train engineer, Murgatroyd, was standing at the bar talking to Constable Leard, Frank's police officer. He had a glass of spirits in his shaking hands.

"Calm down, man," Constable Leard said. "Tell me exactly what you saw. I need to telegraph for help and the more details I have, the better."

"It was like a wall of rock! Swept those poor sods at the tipple into oblivion, I saw it! We was just lucky to get the train out in time. The rocks followed us down, took out the east bridge. There won't be no getting back that way."

"What about the mine itself? Could you see if it collapsed?" asked the policeman.

"Couldn't tell. The entrance is buried, that's for sure, but whether it collapsed? I just couldn't say."

"Nathalie!" shrieked a voice from behind her. Nathalie whirled about, and was caught up in a huge hug. It was Abby, still in her nightdress, curling rags sprouting out from her head in all directions. Nathalie couldn't help herself; she pointed at Abby's head and began to laugh. Abby, in turn, pointed to Nathalie's head and laughed even harder.

Nathalie had forgotten; her mother had curled her hair that evening as well. She had wanted to look so beautiful to meet Helena. Her laughter caught in her throat, and the panic in her stomach gripped once more. Helena! Where was the train?

Nathalie handed her small charges to a surprised Abby and turned to the bar. The engineer and the policeman were gone. She rushed outside, but there was not a man about. Everyone was on the field side, helping. She swallowed hard. The train would be fine; it would have to be. The slide probably didn't cover the tracks. Even if it did, the railway had ways of communicating with other stations. They would be able to stop the train. Wouldn't they?

CHAPTER 13
The Spokane Flyer

ONSTABLE LEARD AND ENGINEER MURGATROYD
returned to the station. The brakemen,
Choquette and Lowes, were badly shaken, and
the spirits Murgatroyd brought back from the hotel were
welcome. The three trainmen tried to piece together as
much information as they could for Leard, but in the
dark it was impossible for anyone to judge the magnitude
of the slide. Shaking his head, Leard tried the telegraph
line. The line to the east was dead. Clearly the slide had
knocked out the telegraph poles in that direction. Leard
tried the west, and was able to connect to Cranbrook, the
next major town in that direction. The telegraph sent the
first news of the slide to the outside world.

Meanwhile, the three trainmen looked grimly at
one another. "If the lines to the east are out, then the

slide has taken out the eastern tracks as well," said Murgatroyd quietly.

"The Flyer is due in when?" asked Lowes. The stationmaster looked grim. "Right now," he replied. Immediately, Sid Choquette got to his feet. He pulled on his sweater, then his coat, and sat down to lace his boots.

"You coming?" he asked Lowes.

"I'd better," replied Lowes. The brakemen bundled up, then turned at the door. "Can you tell which way's east in this dust?"

The station master came to the door and pointed. "That'd be the way," he said. He shook both their hands. "Good luck." And Choquette and Lowes disappeared into the dark.

"You think we'll find the train?" asked Lowes, as the two men began to climb the boulders that blocked the way.

"We got to," replied Choquette. "The Spokane Flyer's a passenger train. If we don't find it, they'll run right into the slide in the dark. They won't have a chance."

With that in mind, the two men struggled up and over the rocks. They fumbled their way forward in the dark, feeling their way. Some boulders were as big as a house and simply too immense to climb. The men had to grope their way around these monsters, inch by inch. Their lanterns barely penetrated the dust cloud, and were of practically no use at all. The rocks were hot, still steaming from their wild ride down the mountainside. As the two men twisted and turned to find a passable route through the boulders, they lost all sense of direction.

Lowes started to choke on the dust. "I can't breathe in this stuff!" They both stopped and wrapped their handkerchiefs around their faces. "Maybe that'll help," suggested Choquette. "We gotta keep going."

They went on. In places the rocks shifted under them, giving them little purchase. Choquette found that he needed to pull the sleeves of his long underwear over his hands to protect them from the heat of the rocks. It was the coldest part of the night, but sweat was pouring down the faces of both men as they laboured forward. Lowes sat down to take a rest.

"No time, Lowes," warned Choquette. "We gotta keep going."

THEY STARTED AGAIN. "We gotta keep going" became a chant in their minds. They ignored the cuts and bruises, the tight choking sensation in their chests, and the dust that filled their eyes. They thought only of that train, hurtling towards disaster in the dark. And then Lowes fell.

One of the boulders shifted as he put his weight on it, and as he reached out for something solid to steady himself, Lowes found only air. His leg buckled and he sat down hard, starting a miniature landslide all around him. Choquette called out to him, and Lowes waved his lantern weakly.

"I'm sorry, Sid. It's my ankle; it twisted when I went down. You gotta go on without me. I'll be too slow."

"I can't leave you here in the middle of nowhere!"

"You got no choice, buddy. I'll be fine, a little cold maybe, but I sure won't die. And those folks out there just might. So go, and hurry!"

Choquette took off one of his sweaters and gave it to Lowes. "I'm just about dying of the heat right now anyway. Take this. If you don't make it back before me, I'll send somebody. Promise."

"I'll be fine. Just go!"

And Choquette went. He turned his back on his friend and climbed the next boulder. And the next. And the next. It seemed the rocks would never end. Choquette was finally getting a sense of just how great a disaster had just occurred. And how much more likely it was to become an even greater disaster if he couldn't warn the train on time.

Choquette wrapped his sleeves around his hands again, and kept climbing.

CHAPTER 14
Making Plans

NATHALIE AND ABBY HAD SET UP A MAKE-shift creche in the small salon beside the bar of the Imperial Hotel. Along with their tiny, lost "wanderers," they had collected five other children, dropped off by adults needed elsewhere. But in spite of their efforts to entertain the little ones with songs and games, all the children were fractious.

"It's no use," sighed Abby. "They're tired and frightened. We should probably just try to get them to sleep." Nathalie nodded. She went to find her mother, who had the keys to the hotel's linen press. Keys in hand, Nathalie collected a few blankets and pillows, then the two girls made a cozy nest for their charges in a quiet corner of the salon. But still the children would not sleep. The noise from the bar was getting louder and louder. Nathalie went to the door of the salon to see what was causing the commotion.

Mr. Chambers, the president of the Board of Trade, had called a meeting. The bar was full of grown-ups, a few women and about twenty or thirty men who had just arrived to help. Constable Leard was standing beside the president.

"Listen, can everybody hear me?" called out Mr. Chambers, in a loud voice. "For those of you who just got here, we're going to bring you up to date as best we can. We got about another hour until daylight, and that's when the real work begins. A lot of the men are already over the creek, and they'll need relieving. And we got other problems besides that. We got to have us a plan, and we got to have rescue teams ready for action at first light. First up, we're going to hear from Constable Leard."

The crowd shuffled back to give the constable some space. "The telegraph lines are out to the east, but the western lines are operating. We've already sent a message to Cranbrook asking for help. But that help will take at least a day or more to get here, so right now it's up to us."

"As I see it, we got three problems. The first are the rail lines to the east. If the telegraph is out, then so are the rail lines. The Spokane Flyer is on the way in from Lethbridge, but we already dealt with that. Two of the CPR brakemen are on their way to flag down the train. That's the best we can do for those folks."

Nathalie felt her stomach clench. When she looked up, she caught sight of her mother standing in the doorway of the kitchen, clutching the edge of her apron with one hand and covering her mouth with the other. Nathalie willed her mother to look her way, to smile to show her that it was going to be all right. Her mother did not look over.

"The second problem is the trapped miners."

Nathalie caught her breath. Without a father or a brother in the mines, she had forgotten that men worked all night long in the mine. Could they have survived?

"Do you know for sure they're still alive?" called out a worried voice.

"Ma'am, right now we don't know nothing for sure. But we have here the mining engineer," Constable Leard pulled a man from behind him, "and he'll be talking to you next about what we can do for the miners."

The mining engineer was clearly uncomfortable in front of the crowd. His voice was so quiet that Nathalie could hardly hear what he was saying. She wasn't sure she wanted to hear anyway. The bits that came through were not encouraging. It sounded like the rockslide had dammed Gold Creek, and the creek was backing up and flooding the air shafts in the mine. The mine entrance was completely gone, covered by a whole mountain of limestone rocks. It didn't sound very hopeful to Nathalie. She didn't want to even imagine what it might feel like to be buried inside a mountain.

The mining engineer finished talking, and left with a large number of the men. Nathalie guessed that they were going to put together a rescue plan, and she wished them all the luck in the world. All of a sudden, she felt that she should run to the bridge over Gold Creek and make that very important wish properly. But for all she knew, the wishing bridge might not even still be there. Nathalie shivered. Everything felt so wrong.

Mr. Chambers was back. "So that's the train, and the mine. The last area of concern is the slide itself, over the other side of the creek. Now, most of the men have been over there for the last hour and we're waiting for a report back so that..."

As if on cue, the door of the bar flew open and the empty space was filled with a huge apparition. It was black all over, with a dusting of white on top. Its hands were torn and bleeding. Nathalie and Abby stared with wide eyes. It looked like one of the creatures from Andy's stories, or Nathalie's ogre, come to life. Then the apparition ran those torn hands through its hair and Nathalie knew, all of a sudden, that it was Toby. No apparition, just Toby, a little boy in a man's body.

Every eye was on him. Toby swayed, just a little. "We need...they need..."

Before he could get any more words out, there was a deluge of questions. "How bad is it?" "Are there any houses left standing?" "What's on fire?" "Are there many dead?"

Toby swayed a bit more, then half fell into a nearby chair. "Give the lad some room! Quiet now!" shouted Mr. Chambers.

"Now, son, what is it they need?"

Toby looked up slowly. "They need blankets – for stretchers, you know? And more lanterns. We can hear them crying, but we can't see them..."

There was quiet in the bar.

"And bandages. Lots of bandages." With that, Toby buried his head in his hands and burst into tears.

CHAPTER 15
Inside the Mine

DEEP INSIDE THE MINE, WILLIAM Warrington groaned in pain. The tunnels had stopped rolling and heaving, but he knew the situation was precarious. Whether it had been an explosion or a collapse, all the miners were in grave danger. Warrington called out, hoping that he wasn't alone.

He wasn't. The other men followed Warrington's voice to the tunnel where he lay. There they gently freed him from under the beam, straightened his leg as best they could, then strapped it with lengths of timber and strips of cloth ripped from their shirts. It was a horribly painful process, but it had to be done. Then the miners took stock of the rest of the injuries.

Most of them had fared better than Warrington, receiving only cuts and bruises during the violent shaking of the mountain. As for Charlie, he was nowhere to be found. "Perhaps the mountain swallowed him up," mused one of the Welshmen. "Maybe Napi took him," said Halfpint glumly. At another time, his comment would have made them laugh. But it didn't tonight.

All of the seventeen miners of the night shift, with the exception of Warrington, who couldn't walk, made their way to the entrance of the mine. Assembling there, they looked at the destruction with panic. There was no entrance left. The timbers that had supported the door were crushed to the size of toothpicks. The doorway was completely sealed by rock, and how deep the rocks lay no one could even imagine. There would be no escape there.

Chapman collected his thoughts. As foreman, he felt responsible for his miners, even though he knew in his heart that he alone could not save them. What he could do was try to prevent panic, so they could think. Or not think. Chapman wanted to keep his men busy so they wouldn't have time to dwell on the fact that they just might die that night.

"I want you working in teams of two. Each pair will take one light between them, to save fuel. We'll go down the main tunnel. I'm sending a pair down each of the side tunnels. Take a look at the damage, and explore any new openings or holes that might lead us out. We'll meet back here in an hour. Warrington will be home base."

Leaving Warrington where he was with one lamp for company, the other men spread out, looking for an escape. Their best bet lay below the main entrance. There was a second tunnel that ran under the main tunnel. It was used to provide fresh air for the mine. Between the two tunnels was a "man-way," a smaller connecting tunnel that acted like a stairway between them. Halfpint Jones scrambled down the man-way into the lower tunnel, and was horrified to find it filling with water. As the mining engineer had seen from the outside, the slide had dammed the creek. Climbing back up to the main tunnel, Halfpint shook his head. That escape was blocked.

An hour later, the miners congregated back around Warrington to think things through. Each pair reported.

"Tunnel Two is blocked about forty feet along. No new openings."

"Same for Tunnel Three."

Shorty Dawson broke in. "That new tunnel we was workin' on, past Three, it's open. But it don't go nowhere, except down the man-way to the lower tunnel. And if Halfpint says that's no good, then the new tunnel won't help us none."

They couldn't escape from where they were, and they couldn't go down; that left up as the only possible route. Shorty Dawson, Joseph Chapman, and John Watkins, Ruby's father, teamed up to explore the possibilities. They had to make their way back into the heart of the mountain through the twisted passages for nearly a mile until they came to one of the upper air shafts. These shafts had been drilled nearly straight up to bring air from the surface. But as the three men climbed higher and higher, their worst fears were realized. Disheartened, they made their way back to the group waiting with Warrington.

"Can't be done," said Watkins. "The air shafts are completely blocked. There's no telling how much rock is on top of us."

Chapman was grave. As the most experienced miner of the crew, he had recognized an even greater danger. With the air shafts blocked, the lethal gas created by the coal dust had no outlet to the surface either. The gas, being lighter than air, was rising to the top of the air shafts and accumulating. It was just a matter of time before it exploded. And that was only if the men didn't suffocate first. With no air, their time underground was very limited. He could see the fear in his men's eyes, eyes that stood out big and white against faces black with coal dust.

Caught between rising floodwaters below and lethal gas above, the miners had no choice.

Chapman spoke. "Here's the plan. We go back to the main entrance and dig. We got to remember that the folks from town will be digging on the other side, because they'll assume we'll be at the entrance. It only makes sense. Let's get to it, and get ourselves out!"

After a half-hearted cheer to bolster their confidence, they made their way back to the main entrance of the mine, raised their picks and shovels, and started digging. Not a single miner dared wonder out loud if there was anyone in Frank left alive to rescue them.

CHAPTER 16
Nathalie's Plan

TOBY'S DRAMATIC ENTRANCE INTO THE HOTEL bar had the grown-ups buzzing. Some were rushing about putting together the items he had requested. Others were putting their heads together, making more plans, Nathalie guessed. Toby was left, all alone, filthy, on the chair that he had fallen into. Toby might not know the first thing about history, but right now he was helping save their friends. Once again leaving the children with Abby, Nathalie crossed the bar and crouched down beside him.

"Toby," she said softly. "Toby?"

Slowly, Toby raised his dirty face. "Oh Nattie," he said, his tears making tracks down his cheeks. "It's so awful! There's just nothin' left over there! I can't go back, I can't...."

"Is there something I can do?" asked Nathalie. "I know the grown-ups have plans, but right now, you and me, is there anything we can do?"

All of a sudden Toby grinned. "You'll be lookin' for Lester, right? I bet you thought nobody knew, eh? That you were sweet on him and all. But I knew! I'm not stupid!"

Nathalie blushed. "I know you're not, Toby. I used to think you were lazy, but not any more. Right now you're helping, and that makes you a hero. And I want to help too. Please take me, Toby!"

Nathalie's words were just what Toby needed. He lumbered up from his chair. "What they really need are scouts. People who can, you know, listen to the rocks in case somebody's calling from underneath. You and me, we can do that. All we gotta do if we hear somebody is call the searchers and they'll come right over and start diggin'. But they'll need lanterns. Can you get some?"

Nathalie said, "Wait here!" and rushed off to find her mother. "Does the hotel have any more lanterns?" she asked in a rush.

"No, Constable Leard just came and got them all. Why?"

"Can I go home and get ours?"

"Nathalie, what are you up to?" asked her mother worriedly. "Don't be thinking you can move that slide all by yourself. I know you're worried about your friends, but you'll just be in the way."

"Toby's been over there, Mama. He says they need trackers, people who can listen for voices under the rocks. I can do that, Mama! I wouldn't get in the way, I'd be helping. And I wouldn't be digging, not one bit, because I know I'm not strong enough for that. I have to *do* something, Mama!"

Just then, the proprietor rushed in and grabbed her mama by the arm. "Mrs. Vaughan, we need you to..." As he steered her down the hall, Nathalie's mama looked over her shoulder and called out, "Just be careful, you hear?"

Taking that as permission, Nathalie ran back to Toby. "We can get the lanterns from my house. Come on, hurry!"

CHAPTER 17
The Search for the Flyer

SID CHOQUETTE WAS EXHAUSTED. THERE WERE blisters on his hands from the hot rocks and his lungs were burning from all the limestone dust. Surely, he thought to himself, it's too late. He felt as if he had been scrambling over rocks for hours, too many hours. The Spokane Flyer had not been that far away when the slide hit; it must have long since barrelled right into the wall of rock. That is, if it hadn't been buried in the first place.

Perhaps that was it. Maybe he had actually climbed right over the train, which lay beneath the monstrous boulders with all the people trapped inside. As soon as the thought came into his head, Choquette's tired brain insisted that it was true. They were all dead. All of them. There was nothing he could do. He might as well go back and get Lowes; at least then he could say he'd rescued one person that night. He just needed to rest a bit, and then he would go back....

Choquette sat down on a flattened rock. Funny, he thought to himself, the rocks have fallen into the shape of a throne. Here I sit, king of disaster. My kingdom, buried. My people, dead. But my throne remains. I am King!

Exhausted, Choquette tried to chase the wild thoughts from his head. He was behaving like Old Bill after a little too much of the "demon rum," as Bill called his favourite drink. He was sitting on a pile of rocks, that was all. Not a throne. Not a tomb. But there was no question that pile of rocks was going to be big trouble when the Spokane Flyer came barrelling into it. It was really too bad that he wasn't going to be able to stop the train in time. It was just too far. There were too many rocks.

Now that he had stopped climbing, Choquette began to feel a bit chilled. The icy air worked its way down his neck, and into the sleeves of his jacket. His toes felt numb. He promised himself he would just sit a minute before turning back to find Lowes. As he sat, he imagined the train. Would the passengers see the rocks before they hit? Or would the crash be a complete surprise? What about the engineer?

Oh, he'd see it all right. But not in time. He would look up into the darkness and see a piece of the sky that just didn't look right. He would peer forward into the night, wondering what it was that was bothering him, while the train hurtled closer and closer every second.

And all of a sudden it would come to him — "There's something on the tracks!" — and he would leap for the brake and pull with all his might, but it wouldn't be fast enough and the strange bit of darkness would get closer and closer and the violent braking would throw the passengers from their seats and they would start shouting, "What's the matter?"

But they wouldn't be able to see the strange darkness, so they wouldn't know what was just in front of them, and the children would begin to cry because they wouldn't understand — oh, the children! — and the engineer would realize that it was too late and he wouldn't even have time to leap from the locomotive.

And it would hit with a horrible crash and then all the cars behind would accordion into the slide with a horrible squealing and twisting of metal and the lucky passengers would die right away but others would just be badly hurt or trapped, but they wouldn't be able to move and that would be horrible because the boiler would start a fire and they would be burned to death, horribly, slowly, with no one to help....

Fire. Choquette peered into the darkness. There was no fire. The train hadn't hit; there was still time!

Choquette leapt to his feet and plunged forward. His first step took him out of his "throne" and the second launched him into mid-air. There was nothing there. Falling hard onto his knees, Choquette felt his forward momentum push him into a somersault and he tumbled, head over heels, down a steep bank of scree. Landing with a thud, he slowly and painfully tested every part of his body. Nothing was broken, thank goodness. He was bruised and cut, perhaps, but all in all, he had been lucky. Carefully Choquette got to his feet, and for the first time in ages felt solid ground beneath him.

He had reached the end of the slide.

Just then, he heard a train whistle echo through the night. The Flyer! Bruises notwithstanding, Choquette picked up his lantern and ran as he had never run before.

CHAPTER 18
Across Gold Creek

NATHALIE FOLLOWED THE BOUNCING LIGHT that came from Toby's lantern. She was afraid that if she lost sight of it in the cloud of dust, she would be too disoriented to find her way back. None of the familiar landmarks were in the places she remembered. The wishing bridge over Gold Creek was gone, which wasn't a surprise. What was a surprise was the fact that Gold Creek was no longer a creek, but a lake.

As she scrambled behind Toby, as he picked his way through the shallowest parts of the rising water towards the other side, Nathalie gave a quick thought to all the wishes that the bridge had collected. Where were they now? Probably gone forever. The knot in her stomach clenched again as she thought of the many wishes she had made for a brother or a sister.

Then she pushed all thoughts of Helena out of her mind. She couldn't think of the train right now.

Nathalie caught up with Toby. "This isn't so bad," she said, looking around. "There's not many rocks."

"Just wait," replied Toby grimly.

About two hundred yards down the path, it ended all of a sudden. The path was completely swallowed up by a wall of rock so high Nathalie couldn't see the top. It looked as if some great creature had drawn a line down the mountain and decreed that no rocks could fall outside the line. Maybe the ogre from her story, Nathalie thought. Had that only been a few hours ago? Or maybe it was Napi, from Andy's story. Had he finally decided to punish the miners for cutting holes in his house? Nathalie shook her head. These were all thoughts that she needed to shut away right now. This was not a story. This was real, no matter how much she might wish otherwise.

Nathalie followed Toby on a diagonal across the rocks. As they inched ever higher up the wall, she felt fear clench her belly. She felt as if she were entering the ogre's territory, and would soon be at its mercy. Where was Charlie now, she tried to joke with herself. Charlie could save me. He could save all of us! But the joke wasn't funny. For all she knew, Charlie was trapped in the mine.

All of a sudden they were on top, and Nathalie nearly fell through the Bansemers' roof. She looked around in confusion. This was not where the house was supposed to be!

"Frances! Frances!"

"Nathalie?" Frances called weakly from somewhere to Nathalie's right. "I'm here!"

With the light of her lantern, Nathalie found Frances and made her way to her side. The girls fell into each other's arms. "What happened to your house?"

"The rocks pushed it off the foundation. The searchers couldn't use any of the doors or windows because of all the mud and rocks and stuff, so they cut a hole in the roof. We're okay, though, all of us. We're so lucky, Nathalie!"

Just then one of the searchers came to lead the Bansemer family to safety across the rising creek. "Nathalie, you have to find the others! Ruby and Jessie and Lester and all the rest – you have to keep looking!" Frances began to cry.

"Don't worry, Frances, I'll keep looking. I promise!"

But as Nathalie looked around, the task seemed impossible. There was destruction everywhere. Fires were burning from the coal stoves that had been upset. People were crying. Nathalie felt like crying too, but remembered why she was there. One of her friends was safe, and that was a start. But not the end. Nathalie began to make her way towards the next cottage.

Jessie's house wasn't buried, but it had been cut in two. The top half was completely gone, who knew where. Just then Toby called out from the Ennis house. "There's somebody under here!"

Lanterns from all directions began to bob in the direction of his voice. Mr. Ennis had just scrambled out from under the rocks, and he was trying to pull his wife up behind him. But she was caught under a beam from the crushed house. Searchers worked to free her, causing a small mudslide with their efforts. Mr. Ennis kept tight hold of his wife's hand so as not to lose her in the mud, and finally the beam shifted. Everybody pulled and out she came, completely covered in mud. In her arms was her baby, Gladys.

"She's not crying," Mrs. Ennis said anxiously. "Something's wrong. Help her!"

One of the searchers held his lantern close and Mrs. Ennis carefully unwrapped Gladys. The baby was blue. She wasn't breathing. Mrs. Ennis reached into her mouth and took out a great clod of mud. The baby choked, then began to cry. Everyone cheered.

In no time at all the searchers had dug up the other three Ennis children, all of whom were badly bruised but alive. Mrs. Ennis's brother was rescued from the back bedroom. "There was something odd, I tell you," he told the rescuers. "I was thrown and I landed on something real soft. Something that shouldn't have been there."

Searchers continued to dig, and found Mrs. Watkins, Ruby's mother, from next door. She was badly hurt, but also alive. How she had survived being flung from one house into the next and landing *under* a resident of that house no one could even imagine. Especially since there was nothing left of her own house.

There were cheers celebrating the rescue of the Ennis family and Mrs. Watkins. But not from Nathalie. She was happy that Mrs. Watkins was safe, but where was Ruby?

ABOUT ONE HUNDRED FEET AWAY, *two shapes emerged from the rocks. They thought they could hear voices, but in the dark and the dust it was hard to tell where the voices were coming from. The two shapes held hands, and began to stumble towards the voices. But then there was silence. It was as if the great cloud of dust had closed them in and shut out all sound.*

Ruby squeezed her brother Thomas's hand. "I'm scared," she said. Thomas squeezed back.

"Me too."

Off they went in the darkness. Any direction was better than where they stood. The rocks had to end somewhere. Didn't they?

CHAPTER 19
Hope...and Despair

AFTER THE SUCCESS AT THE ENNIS CABIN, the searchers were buoyed. Nathalie and Toby picked their way back towards the Leitch home and one of the searchers called for silence. All listened. The silence persisted.

A man called out.

"Leitch! Are you there, man?"

Nothing.

Picks and shovels were lifted. Day was breaking, but a day so weak that it did not seem able to push away the night before. It was almost better working in the dark, thought Nathalie. Seeing was worse than imagining, she found, for it left less room for hope. And she had to hold on to hope, even if there was just a shred. She listened as hard as she could.

The pit boss of the mine found a way through the collapsed walls of the house and crawled room to room. First the seachers found Jessie's mother and father, buried in their bed. They were dead. Then they found two of Jessie's brothers. They had been crushed by a wall. Nathalie's heart was in her mouth. She didn't want to see; she couldn't! Then they found Jessie and her sister Rosemary.

They were lying in their double bed, with a ceiling joist wedged between them. "I'm cold," said Rosemary. "Please get us out!" cried Jessie. The searchers cheered. Nathalie burst into tears.

But they couldn't find the other two boys. And baby Marion was gone.

IT WAS SUCH A TINY CRY. *The picks and shovels made so much noise that nobody could hear. They thought they were listening, but they didn't hear.*

JESSIE AND ROSEMARY were gently lifted out of the remains of their home. Nathalie rushed to hug them. One of the searchers held out a bottle to the girls.

"Thank goodness!" exclaimed Jessie. "I really need to wash all that mud out of my mouth." With that, she took a big drink from the bottle. Her eyes grew huge, the liquid sprayed everywhere and Jessie choked and choked.

"What's the matter?" asked Nathalie, as she pounded her friend on the back.

"That wasn't water," Jessie replied in a strangled voice. "Yech!"

"That's brandy," said the searcher. "In case you go into shock or something. Now come along with me, and I'll take you back to town so Doc Malcolmson can take a look at you two."

Thank goodness for the brandy, thought Nathalie, as she waved goodbye to Jessie. At least it made us laugh for a minute. She didn't think there would be much laughing for Jessie any more. Why? *Why* did this have to happen?

THE CRY WAS CUT OFF *by a gulp and a sniffle. She was so cold. She wanted her mama. Why didn't her mama come?*

THE SEARCHERS NOW BEGAN to spread out to the next cottage. As the day grew lighter and lighter, Nathalie was forced to see more and more of the destruction. She looked ahead to Lester's house. It was in ruins. No one could have survived that, she thought hopelessly to herself. Lester was gone. That was it. Ruby too. She hung behind as the search team extracted the bodies of Lester's mother and stepdad. They found no one else, and they moved to the next house. She had to turn her head away. Past Lester's house, Ruby's was nothing more than firewood. Past that, the Clarke's house was just plain gone. She couldn't help here. She couldn't stay here. Nathalie wanted her mother.

CHAPTER 20
A Tiny Cry

L ESTER SLOWLY BECAME CONSCIOUS. HE COULD
*see the searchers at the next house, and called out. But
they were too far away. And he couldn't move. Something
was holding him down. He tried to twist a bit, and then he saw.
A piece of wood from the house had gone through his side, pin-
ning him to his bed. Lester got a firm hold on the stake, took a
deep breath, and broke it in two. And then he fainted.*

NATHALIE TURNED AROUND and began to make her
way back through the rubble towards town. She told
herself she still wanted to help, that there were useful
things for her to do back in Frank. But she knew she
was leaving because she was afraid. And she was disappointed in herself. Again.

She passed the remains of the Ennis house, then clambered around the Leitch house. Then she stopped. Had she heard something? Nathalie held herself perfectly still, hardly even breathing. She listened with every bit of her being. She forgot that she was afraid. And she heard it again.

It was a tiny cry, she was sure of it. She climbed into the ruined Leitch house, just as the pit boss had done. She inched through the rooms, looking with apprehension at the crumbling walls all around her. Every few feet she stopped and held herself perfectly still. She couldn't hear it any more. The cry had disappeared.

Nathalie retraced her steps and crawled back out to the rocks. And she listened. There it was again!

"Hello?" she called. She waited.

"Hello?"

Nathalie moved ten paces to her right, and listened. Nothing. She moved back to her first spot, then moved ten paces to the left. Nothing. Back to the center. This time she went up the hill. And there it was! It was a baby, she was sure, maybe Marion, Jessie's little sister! Just in case, she called out to her.

"Marion? Is that you honey? It's Nathalie. Can you say Nathalie?"

Nathalie stayed stock still.

"Nattie?" came a wispy voice, just off to her left. Nathalie crawled on her hands and knees, not even noticing the sharp rocks. "Marion, say Nattie again."

Half an hour later, Nathalie was still calling out to the baby, but the baby was no longer answering her frantic calls. Maybe she had fallen asleep, or worse. Who knew if she was badly hurt? Desperately Nathalie crawled this way and that. It was just that there was so much rubble and it all looked the same!

With tears of exhaustion and frustration rolling down her cheeks, Nathalie kept crawling. Until all of a sudden a tiny fist reached out and grabbed one of the mucky rags in Nathalie's hair.

"Funny Nattie!" said the mudball that was attached to the fist. With the tears still streaming down her face, Nathalie burst out laughing as she cradled Marion in her lap. No wonder she had missed her; the child was covered in mud and blended completely with the debris around her. But she *had* found her, all the same. Nathalie cuddled the baby close and rested for a moment, rubbing the tiny hands and feet to warm them up.

LESTER'S EYES OPENED AGAIN. *Where was he? He still wasn't sure what had happened, but he knew he needed help. Holding the remains of the stake so that it didn't further open the wound, he sat up carefully, then gingerly stood. He could do it. He could get himself out. Slowly and carefully, Lester began to make his way, half-walking and half-crawling, towards the morning lights of Frank. He didn't even notice that the slide had ripped the pajamas right off his body, leaving him stark naked.*

AFTER A SHORT REST, Nathalie bundled the baby inside her coat to keep her safe. She was going to need both hands to navigate the rocks. Carefully, she too made her way towards Frank, anxious to see the look on Jessie's face when she saw her baby sister safe and sound. Nathalie had completely forgotten that she had been afraid.

CHAPTER 21
No Way Up, No Way Down

ALTHOUGH THE SUN WAS RISING OVER FRANK, it was still pitch dark in the mine. For hours the men had been using their tools to try to make their way through the debris at the collapsed entrance. It was terribly difficult, and confusing as well. There was so much rock that it was hard to keep steady in any direction. The miners kept losing any sense of the way they were meant to be digging. At first the men sang to keep their spirits up. But as the hours wore on with no real success, the singing stopped. A short time after that, the work stopped too. The seventeen miners found places along the tunnel walls and sank down, exhausted.

"Do you think we'll be getting out of here?" asked Dan McKenzie, in a conversational tone of voice that masked the fear that he felt.

"Likely not," replied Shorty. "Air's getting a bit thin, don't you think?"

The two sounded as if they were having a chat over their lunch pails, or talking about the weather. Death was something a miner looked in the face every time he went into the dark. But it was always something that was going to happen to someone else. When it came, it would come quickly, in an explosion or a cave-in. Not a man there had imagined waiting for death, trapped inside a mountain that refused to let them go. McKenzie and Shorty were trying their best to stay calm, for if they could not do that, all would be lost.

One of the Welshmen began to weep, quietly, in the dark. "Belle," he whispered. "Forgive me for leaving you." A young miner jumped to his feet, tore his hard hat from his head and began to beat it against the wall.

'I'm only twenty years old!" he screamed. "This isn't fair!" He continued banging his hat until Ruby's father, John Watkins, pulled him back from the wall.

"That'll be enough of that now," he said softly. "Be still now, lad. Be still."

Watkins sat the boy down and squeezed his shoulder. Then he made his way to the place where Warrington lay.

"How are you doing? Need a sip of water?" he asked.

Warrington nodded gratefully. "I'll be all right as soon as we make it out of here," he said, "and a sip of water would be a fine thing."

Watkins unscrewed the flask attached to his belt and held Warrington's head so that he could drink. Then he sat down beside the injured man. "I've been thinking about my family," said Watkins. "I imagine you have as well."

"Can't stop thinking about them. It's hard to imagine what may be out there. Reckon it was a landslide?"

"Probably. If it had been an explosion, we wouldn't be sitting here talking about it. My guess is that part of Turtle Mountain came down and is lying on top of the mine."

"You think it buried the town as well?"

"No way to tell. When I think about Turtle Mountain, I remember there's an overhanging ledge off to the north there. Maybe that's the part that broke off."

The two family men looked at one another. If the ledge was indeed the part that had fallen, then both of their homes − and their families inside − would have been directly in the path of the slide.

There was silence again in the mine; silence except for the steady weeping that came from the Welshman. All of a sudden Joe Chapman, the foreman, stood up.

"What is this?" he bellowed, his words echoing in the tunnel. "We're not dead yet! Think, men! Our lives depend on it. We can't go down, we can't go up, we can't get through the door. So where else can we go?"

More silence. And sighs. After all, where could they go? Then William Warrington's voice spoke out, tight with the pain from his hip, but strong nonetheless. "I've got a family out there I'd like to see again," he said. "What if we dug through the coal?"

Chapman caught on to the idea immediately. "That's it!" he exclaimed. "It's easy to dig through the coal seams. They'll probably take us straight to the surface. We'll know we're going in the right direction, and we'll be able to save our strength a bit, because it won't be as hard as dealing with the rock. Good man, Warrington. That'll be the plan."

With that Chapman organized his miners. They put their heads together and determined, as best they could, where the coal seams were in relation to their position in the tunnel. Chapman sent teams of two back through the tunnels to poke and prod between the roofing timbers to find the nearest coal seam. It was Charlie Farrell who found it, not very far back. Maybe it was possible after all.

But as the teams reassembled, Chapman could see that the little bit of exertion had tired the men far more than it should. That meant that they weren't getting enough air. How could they tackle such a project if they couldn't breathe? Quickly he organized small teams to take turns, before any of the miners had time to panic about their dwindling air supply. It was practical anyway; the coal seam was narrow and could only take two diggers at a time. So as Turtle Mountain slowly squeezed the breath from the miners' lungs, pairs of men took turns trying to poke a hole in the mountain's side.

CHAPTER 22
Nathalie Makes a Wish

NATHALIE HAD NEVER BEEN SO GRATEFUL for her heavy winter boots. Between the rocks and the gloom and the baby under her coat, Nathalie had to consider every single step she took. Without the boots, she was sure that she would never have made it off the slide. But here she was, standing on the path once more. Before going on, she turned and looked behind her at the wall of jumbled boulders behind her. She shuddered, turned back to the path, and pressed on.

Although the sun was up, the cloud of limestone dust made visibility poor. So Nathalie was surprised when she all of a sudden stepped into a puddle. Looking down, she saw that it wasn't a puddle at all, but a small lake, stretching in front of her. Surely this wasn't Gold Creek? It had not been so long ago that Toby had led her through the creek on their way to the slide. The water, dammed by the rocks, had been rising, but they could still make their way across. Nathalie could tell by looking that not only was the creek five times wider, but it was much too deep for her boots as well. Sighing, she sat down on the path.

Marion had actually fallen asleep from the warmth of Nathalie's body under the thick winter coat. But as soon as Nathalie stopped moving, the baby woke up and started to cry. Nathalie had no doubt that on top of being tired, cold, muddy, and possibly hurt, she was probably also hungry, and from the smell, wearing a dirty diaper. Unfortunately, she couldn't do a thing about any of those problems right that moment. So Nathalie lifted the baby out of her coat and sat her down on the path.

"So, Marion," said Nathalie conversationally, "how would you like to go swimming? No? You think it's too cold, maybe? I don't know; I've always liked swimming in April. No, that's not true. The water will be freezing. Maybe you'd like to ride on my shoulders? I'm sure you would. I would if I were you. But then I'm not the one with the dirty diaper, am I? But of course that's not your fault; you're only a baby, after all. So here's my plan. I'm going to take off your diaper and clean you up as best I can with my handkerchief. Then like it or not we have to put your nightdress back on you, without your diaper. And you're going to try real hard to remember that you're not wearing a diaper, right, Marion?!"

Marion stopped crying. She looked up at Nathalie, clearly not understanding a word that was being said, but calmed by the singsong of Nathalie's voice. "Dirty," said Marion, pointing to her bottom. "Off."

Nathalie started to laugh. "Off it is, then," she said, and proceeded to clean the baby up as well as she could. Then Nathalie took off her boots and stockings and looped them around her neck. She hoisted the baby to her shoulders, amid squeals of laughter from Marion. "We're off!"

Nathalie stepped into the water and nearly dropped the baby. The water was beyond icy; it was so cold that Nathalie's back teeth hurt. But there was no other way to get back to town, and the water was rising fast. It was already up to her knees. So on she went. It only took a very few minutes for Nathalie's feet and legs to become completely numb, and that actually made the going easier, as she couldn't feel a thing. She concentrated on putting one foot in front of the other, just as she had done with the rocks, all the while keeping the ever-larger lights of Frank directly ahead of her. One foot, then another. And another. And another. And then her toe caught, and she went down.

Nathalie grabbed for Marion, who got wet but didn't go under. The baby started to scream with the cold. Nathalie struggled upright, holding the baby in her arms, but it was difficult, as her coat now weighed about a hundred pounds. At least it felt like a hundred pounds.

Still holding Marion in her arms, Nathalie reached down to extricate her foot from whatever it was that was lurking under the water. She tugged, and up came a broken piece of wood. Nathalie looked at it carefully, then caught her breath. It was part of the railing from the wishing bridge. Had it caught her foot on purpose? Was she meant to make a wish?

Standing up to her knees in frigid water in the middle of a small, ever-rising lake with a wet, crying baby in her arms, Nathalie gripped tightly to the bit of wood. This wish had to be important. It had to be for everyone. It had to be for all the people waiting to be found. It had to help those who had lost their families or friends. It had to help the train.

Nathalie wondered if one wish could do all that. She wondered if she was strong enough to make the wish. Well, even if she wasn't, Nathalie reasoned, there was no one else to make it. She was the only one with a piece of the bridge, so she had to try.

The water was too cold to stop for the proper ritual. Nathalie just gripped the piece of railing tightly, and kept putting one foot in front of the other, wishing as she went. Nathalie put her whole heart into the wish. She couldn't even say it in words; the wish was just too big for that. She tried to think of all the people who needed wishes, and what they would need. She wished and wished until she thought her brain would explode. Then she stopped. She was clenching the railing so tightly her fingers felt like they could never uncurl. Nathalie opened her eyes. She'd done what she could.

CHAPTER 23
Lester

HOLDING BOTH THE RAIL AND THE BABY, Nathalie continued across the lake. When she finally reached the other side, she was exhausted. She sat down, put Marion down beside her, and put her shoes and stockings back on. They hardly helped, though; her feet were like blocks of ice. Once more wrapping Marion inside her coat, wet though it was, she looked around to get her bearings. The lights of town were straight ahead. Off to the right, much closer than town, was the Williamson cabin. There were lights glowing in the windows at the Williamsons', and Nathalie considered going there first to borrow a blanket for Marion. As she was deciding, Nathalie caught sight of something odd.

She peered through the haze. She was sure it was a person, someone in trouble. Nathalie moved closer. The person was staggering from side to side as if he were hurt. Nathalie went closer still. It was Lester! And now she realized what had seemed so odd from a distance. He was naked!

"Lester! Lester! Are you all right?" she cried.

"Nattie? Is that you? Oh, please don't look!" Lester fell to his knees.

"I'm not looking, I promise. But you can hardly stand! Are you hurt?"

"A little, I think," Lester called back. "I have this piece of wood stuck in my side. And the rocks, they were hard. Nattie, I'm really tired..." Lester slumped even more.

"Lester! Don't fall asleep! You're barely out of the water. Wake up! I'm going for help!"

Nathalie ran as fast as she could to the Williamsons' cabin. Out came Mr. and Mrs. Williamson at a run. Mr. Williamson had just come back from helping fight fires and he was clearly tired, but when he learned that Lester was hurt, he ran to help. He scooped him up in his arms, then hurried back to the cabin.

Mrs. Williamson and Nathalie met him at the door. "He says he's got a stake in his side; we'd better be careful," said Nathalie. Mrs. Williamson took one look at Lester and grabbed the quilt from their bed. Being careful of the wound, they wrapped Lester and put him into a wheelbarrow. Mr. Williamson just didn't have the strength left to carry him all the way into town.

"Take him to Doc Malcolmson's," said Mrs. Williamson. "And be careful! Now, Nathalie dear, why don't you sit down? Let me warm you up, you look all in."

"Thanks, Mrs. Williamson, but I have to get to Doc Malcolmson's too. I have to make sure that Marion's okay." Nathalie unbuttoned her coat. Marion had once more fallen asleep.

"Land sakes, child!" exclaimed Mrs. Williamson. "Wherever did you find her?"

"On a bale of hay on top of the rocks about two hundred feet away from her house," replied Nathalie. "It took me a long time to find her and then I dropped her in the water. I'm going to take her to Doc's, but may I borrow a blanket for her? She's so cold."

"It looks like she's not the only person who got dropped in the water," smiled Mrs. Williamson, looking at Nathalie's sopping coat. "Leave that wet thing here with me. I'll find blankets for the both of you." Mrs. Williamson bustled about. The dry blanket felt like heaven to Nathalie, and she impulsively hugged Mrs. Williamson.

"That baby looks to be doing just fine, so don't you worry," said Mrs. Williamson, as Nathalie said goodbye. "I'll dry out your coat and you can come get it later. You did a good thing here tonight, Miss

Nathalie Vaughan. You should be proud." Mrs. Williamson waved her off.

Nathalie frowned to herself as she started towards Doc Malcolmson's. Mostly she disregarded people when they said that she had done something good. After all, if she was good, wouldn't her grandfather want her? But tonight she wondered. She *had* done something good tonight. Maybe she wasn't a disappointment, and Grandfather just didn't realize it.

That was a new thought.

CHAPTER 24
Feathers

BY THE TIME NATHALIE ARRIVED AT DOC Malcolmson's, a crowd had gathered around the wheelbarrow. Mr. Williamson carefully lifted Lester and took him inside. The only place left to put him was the dining room table. The surgery was full, and Doc had opened up his house for the overflow. Volunteers quickly cleared the table and put down a blanket, and Lester was laid on top of it.

"The lad lost consciousness on the way over," explained Mr. Williamson. "He's got this awful stake in his side, and I guess the jarring of the barrow over the ruts was mighty painful. But he's breathing still, and not bleeding much. That girl over there," he pointed over to Nathalie, "she found him and came to get us."

Doc looked up. "Nathalie, are you all right?" Nathalie nodded. "Good then," he said, turning back to Lester. "What have we here?" As Doc worked on Lester, Nathalie sank into a chair by the door. She'd made it to safety. Now that she was here, she didn't know what to do. She was exhausted. People were bustling all about and Nathalie hardly even noticed. Her eyes were beginning to close, when Doc shook her awake.

"Nathalie," he said gently. "Are you sure you're not hurt? You look like you've been through a lot."

Nathalie smiled at Doc Malcolmson. He had always been one of her favourite people. Ever since her bout with the measles, it had seemed to Nathalie that Doc had paid special attention to her.

"I'm okay, really, Doc," replied Nathalie, straightening up. "But can you look at the baby? I couldn't really do much for her on the rocks and then I fell in the water and she got wet and I just don't know if she's hurt." Nathalie's words came out all in a rush as she unwrapped Marion and handed her to the doctor.

Doc Malcolmson's eyes grew large. "I don't believe my eyes," he said quietly. "You found her on the rocks?"

"Yes, I went over with Toby to listen for people who were trapped. I heard her crying, but it took me a long time to find her. Please check her, Doc. She has to be all right. Jessie's going to be so sad, and maybe if she sees Marion it will make her feel better."

Doc Malcolmson looked closely at Nathalie. "You know, then, about the Leitch family?"

"I was there," replied Nathalie sadly. "I saw everything."

Doc Malcolmson took Marion over to his big corner desk, which was the only flat surface left that wasn't covered with bandages, ointments, or injured people. Nathalie followed, dragging the wet, dirty blanket behind her. Gently, the doctor moved the baby's arms and legs, checking for broken bones. The movement woke Marion, who immediately started wailing. Doc Malcolmson smiled at Nathalie, who was holding her breath.

"She sounds pretty healthy to me," he laughed. "And no broken bones. Stop worrying, Nathalie. Marion will be fine once we've found her something to eat." Nathalie let her breath out in a rush. Doc Malcolmson looked at her thoughtfully.

"You are a remarkable young lady, Nathalie, that's all I can say," said the Doc, shaking his head. "One thing's for sure, you saved this baby's life. If she'd stayed out all night without being found, she'd probably have frozen to death. And after a bath, some food, and maybe a new diaper," Doc smiled, "she'll be right as rain. But all that can wait. You're right about Jessie. She and Rosemary have just been told about their family. I put them in the back bedroom. Why don't you take Marion in right now?"

Nathalie picked up Marion one more time and made her way through the crowd, glancing over at the nurse who was cleaning Lester's wound so that the Doc could pull the stake out and stitch it shut. She hoped that Lester would stay unconscious for that part. She found the back bedroom and knocked gently on the door. There was no answer. Nathalie pushed open the door and saw Jessie and Rosemary huddled together on the bed. They had been cleaned up, but they looked awful just the same. Their faces were white and their eyes looked too big and too shiny.

"Jessie?"

Jessie looked up. She didn't say a word.

"I've brought you something – someone," said Nathalie, holding out Marion.

Rosemary burst into tears. Jessie sat without moving, but her mouth made a small "o." "Marion, you found Marion," she said in awe. Jessie held out her arms. Nathalie put the baby into Jessie's arms and sat on the end of the bed as the sisters wept together. Poor Jessie. Nathalie couldn't imagine what she would do if she lost her mother. She would be completely alone.

Just then there was an explosion of laughter from the other room.

"What's funny?" asked Jessie. "What on earth can anybody find to laugh about?"

"I'll go see," volunteered Nathalie, wondering if Jessie really wanted to know or just wanted them to stop. Once again, she found a crowd around Lester. Doc had removed the stake. It seemed a miracle that it had only pierced his flesh, and not damaged anything inside his belly. Lester would be just fine, as long as Doc could get the wound completely cleaned out so it didn't become infected. So Doc was painstakingly pulling out slivers of wood, dirt, and tiny rocks with his tweezers.

But as well as those things, which everyone had expected, Doc was pulling out feather after feather! The volunteers guessed that the stake had pinned him to his bed, right through his feather quilt. As Doc removed the feathers, it looked for all the world as if Lester were being plucked, just like a chicken!

Nathalie had to smile. Lester would have a lot of teasing to deal with after this, she knew. But she wouldn't tell a soul that she had seen him naked. Lester could trust her. Nathalie went back to Jessie and Rosemary.

"It's Lester," she said. Her description of Lester's "feathers" brought a small smile to Jessie's lips. Nathalie sat down again on the bed and reached for Jessie's hand.

"Jessie, he's just like you. His mother and stepfather didn't make it either. But he did. And you did. And Rosemary. And Marion is a miracle, Jessie. Little as she is, she called to me to help me find her. This is a horrible, awful slide, but there are some good things to remember. I know it will be hard, but try."

Jessie just stared down at the coverlet, silent tears running down her cheeks. "I can't, Nattie. I just can't," she whispered.

"Jessie, I don't mean right now. But maybe next week, or next month, I want you to imagine Lester being plucked and I want you to smile a little bit. Will you promise to try?"

Slowly Jessie nodded her head, then hugged Nathalie so tightly that she could hardly breathe. The girls stayed together, rocking back and forth, until Jessie stopped crying. Nathalie got up from the bed.

"I have to go now, Jessie. But I'll be back, okay?"

Once more, Jessie nodded. Then, just as Nathalie was leaving, Jessie said, "Nattie? Thank you for Marion."

Nathalie smiled and gently closed the door.

CHAPTER 25
The Vaughan Women

BEFORE LEAVING THE DOC'S HOUSE, NATHALIE looked in on Lester. He was cleaned and stitched, and completely featherless. Nathalie smiled again. He was sleeping now, giving her a chance to really look at him. His nose was a bit crooked and he had a cowlick. She really didn't know why she liked him. But she was ever so glad he was alive. Doc Malcolmson came up behind her and put his big hand on her shoulder.

"He's going to be just fine, young lady. You can stop worrying now. He'll still be around to take you to the school dances, if you like." He smiled.

Nathalie blushed. "He's very nice," she admitted. Somehow it didn't seem wrong saying that to Doc.

"He is, at that," replied Doc. "And so, Miss Nathalie

Vaughan, are you. You're a brave soul. Not everybody could have done what you did tonight."

"But I wasn't brave, Doc," said Nathalie quietly. "The only reason I found Marion was because I was on my way back to town. I wanted to help, but I was too scared. I just couldn't stay. That's not brave."

"Nathalie, that's exactly what being brave is all about. It's about doing what needs to be done even when you're scared. Or when you think the thing that needs to be done is too hard. Or when you think you're not good enough to do it."

Nathalie looked up at the Doc, confused.

Doc Malcolmson went on. "When you were four and had the measles so bad, I thought you would die, just like your father. But you didn't. I couldn't figure out why, you were so sick. I thought to myself, this girl's a fighter. And you were; you got better. After that, I kept a close eye on you, just as I do with all my patients who have been real sick."

Nathalie nodded. "I always wondered why I had more doctor visits than the other kids. You were watching to see if I got sick again, weren't you?"

"That's right. And you didn't. But I worried about you anyway. Sometimes it seemed like there were two Nathalies. One who was a fighter; that was the Nathalie that I knew. But there was another Nathalie, one who thought she was different, maybe not as good as the other children. I don't know why that

Nathalie felt that way, but I do know one thing for sure."

Doc Malcolmson looked Nathalie straight in the eye. "I know that the real Nathalie is the fighter, and that Nathalie can do anything she wants to do. And I hope that when you look into the mirror, you're seeing the strong, smart, brave Nathalie that lives on the inside, not the one that lives on the outside, the one that worries about being good enough.

"You're good enough for anything and anybody, and don't you forget it."

Doc led Nathalie into the kitchen and poured her a steaming cup of cocoa. "You'll be wanting to go see your mother. She's been worried about you. She made this cocoa, you know. She's been sending volunteers with food and hot drinks and bandages all night long. I honestly don't know where we would have been without the Vaughan women tonight. Now, off with you. Wash up, and get some sleep. Doctor's orders. You've earned it."

With that, Doc was off to check on his patients. Left alone, Nathalie sat down hard on a kitchen chair. One of her curling rags, heavy with drying mud, dropped from her hair into her lap. So many once-in-a-lifetime things had happened since her mother had put the rags in her hair. Including Doc's strange words. She would have to think about those words, but not now. She was too tired. She wanted her mother. What had Doc said? She and her mother were "the Vaughan women." With a smile on her dirty face, Nathalie left Doc's and headed towards the hotel.

The dust was settling some, and it was much easier to find her way back. As before, the hotel was very busy. Nathalie checked the salon first. She felt a little guilty about having left Abby alone with all the children. But Abby was fine, stretched out on the blankets, sound asleep, her arms wrapped around two of the littlest ones. Nathalie turned, and came face to face with Ruby.

"I thought it was you!"

"Ruby!"

There were more hugs. Then Nathalie's mother caught sight of her, and rushed over, hugging both the girls at once. "I was so worried! Where were you?"

Nathalie gave a brief account of her night's adventures. Mrs. Vaughan's eyes grew very large as she listened. "Oh, Nattie!" she exclaimed.

Ruby broke into the conversation. "Do you know what I heard? I heard that one of the brakemen climbed right over the rockslide and flagged down the Spokane Flyer, and it stopped in time. Isn't that great?"

Nathalie looked at her mother, who smiled and nodded. "She's right, Nattie. They're fine." Nathalie hugged her mother.

"Didn't I tell you, Mama? That everything would be better than we thought? Frances, Jessie, Ruby, Lester,

Marion, Aunt Sadie, and Helena. And lots more are saved too! When you start with the worst, it just has to get better!"

Her mother smiled, a little sadly. "You're right, sweetheart, but it's not the same for everyone. Many stories are not ending happily. Look." She pointed to the far side of the salon. There sat Lillian Clark, sitting bolt upright in a straight-backed chair. Holding her hand was Ellen Thornley.

"Ellen and John Thornley would have been buried had they stayed in the shoe shop. But they didn't, and they are alive, so it is a happy day for them. But not for Lillian. She is alive because she stayed at the hotel last night. But she lost her mother, her father, and all five of her brothers and sisters. The fact that she was saved gives her no happiness today."

Nathalie looked away from the hurt and the shock in Lillian's eyes. "It's the same for Jessie and Lester," she said.

"Me too," said Ruby, as tears filled her eyes. "My dad is still trapped in the mine."

CHAPTER 26
A Hole in the Mountain

ALARGE RESCUE PARTY HAD BEEN WORKING for hours to free the miners. The engineer had determined the approximate location of the mine entrance, as everyone had agreed it was the most likely place for the miners to be. But it was a desperate situation: the rescue workers didn't know if they were in the right place; they didn't know how deep the rocks lay; they didn't even know if the miners were still alive. But it didn't matter. As long as there was a chance, the rescuers kept digging.

In town, everything was quiet. Most folks had been up all night, many doing hard physical labour, and they needed to rest. Rescue teams were straggling back from the field side of Gold Creek. Sid Choquette had helped his partner back to town and they were both making good use of beds in the Imperial Hotel. Parents came and picked up their children from Abby. Doc Malcolmson had turned the care of his patients over to his day nurse and had fallen asleep in a chair. The Williamsons were sound asleep under their winter coats, as they had given away all their blankets. Toby was safe at home. The Bansemers were staying with friends in town. Mrs. Vaughan and Nathalie went home to sleep, taking Ruby and Thomas with them.

The rescue team at the mine kept digging.

Lillian Clark still sat in her chair. Jessie stared at the wall, rocking Marion.

The sun rose ever higher in the sky.

Old Bill and a few other men made good use of the bar at the Imperial.

The rescue team at the mine kept digging.

Late in the afternoon, the team put down their shovels. They weren't making any progress at all. Exhaustion clouded their eyes, and they were coming to believe that the miners could not still be alive. After all, it had been thirteen hours since the slide. Thirteen hours!

Just then, there was a small rockslide above them. Thinking the worst, the men in the rescue team jumped back, and prepared to run for their lives. But to their surprise, the sight that greeted them as they looked up was Dan McKenzie's head.

"Ho there!" he shouted. "We're up here!"

The rescue team scrambled up the mountainside. Dan Mackenzie's head was sticking up out of a hole in the ground. His face was black with coal dust, but his teeth gleamed white in a broad smile. They were saved! Dan pulled himself out, and reached down a hand to Shorty. By the time Shorty was out, the rescuers had made it to the hole and there were more hands than enough to pull the rest of the miners up. One by one they emerged from the hole, a hole that was about fifty feet higher than the entrance. William Warrington was lifted out on a plank. The miners had successfully dug through the seam of coal, through the rocks and out into the fresh air.

"John, John!" came a shout. "You old codger, I knew you wouldn't stay buried!" The rescuers crowded around; there were hugs, a few tears, some good-natured slaps on the back, and much shouting all around. But John Watkins, William Warrington, and the other miners all had a question in their eyes. Slowly, the crowd of rescuers opened up the circle. The cheers were immediately silenced as the miners looked around them.

"My God," breathed Joe Chapman. The whole north face of the mountain was gone. Smoke drifted in the air from the fires that were still burning. They could see the Imperial Hotel and some of the other establishments that lined the main street of Frank, but there were no buildings on the other side of Gold

Creek. Only rocks, some as big as houses. And the creek wasn't a creek any more; it was a huge lake, a lake that had not existed when the seventeen miners had started their shift the previous night. The scene was incomprehensible.

John Watkins's face was ashen as he looked at the place where his house had been. Rescuers were quick to tell him that his wife was hurt but recovering, and his children were safe. Not so for William Warrington. The pain in his body was nothing to the despair and panic he felt when he looked into the eyes of the men carrying his stretcher. It could not be true. He could not have lost his wife and his three children. He was going to move his family into town and buy a brand new chair for his wife at Leitch's Furniture Store. Surely she would still have a chance to sit in it? But the faces around him told him otherwise. For Warrington, all was lost.

AROUND FIVE O'CLOCK in the afternoon, Nathalie was awakened by a terrific shout. She sat bolt upright in the big bed. What now? she wondered. Haven't we had enough? She got out of bed and went to the window, where she saw an amazing sight. Nathalie dashed back to the bed and gave Ruby a shake.

"Ruby, wake up, wake up! Come and see!" She dragged her friend to the window, and the two girls stood side by side, hardly believing their eyes.

A wagon with a stretcher in it was making its way down Dominion Avenue, surrounded by shouting men, some of them filthy. Sixteen of those men were miners. Every last one of the missing men was safe out of the mine. People were rushing out of their homes, cheering. The men waved. It was like a parade, only better, thought Nathalie. Ruby was laughing through her tears.

"Thomas, Thomas, wake up! Dad's come back!"

CHAPTER 27
Keepsakes

I N THE DAYS THAT FOLLOWED, ROCKS CONTINUED to fall from Turtle Mountain. They didn't fall on anything important, but it was scary just the same. Some people thought that the rocks might start falling on their homes next. Nathalie was almost relieved when the authorities decided that the town had to be evacuated. Everyone was moved to Blairmore, and for nine long days the citizens of Frank watched and waited for another slide to destroy what was left of the town. But the second slide never came, the evacuation was lifted, and the residents of Frank were allowed to go back home.

But not many did. Nathalie's days were filled with goodbyes as her friends moved away. The Bansemer family had already been planning to homestead down the river. The loss of their home just meant that they moved earlier than they had planned. Jessie, Rosemary, and baby Marion went to live with an uncle in Cranbrook. Abby and Ruby and their families left. With the Frank mine closed, their fathers had to find other jobs.

Lester was being sent to live with relatives.

Nathalie had heard that he was going as soon as his wound healed. She had expected it; he had to live with somebody now that his family was gone. What she hadn't expected was the knock on her door late one afternoon.

"Hi, Nathalie," said Lester, who was dressed in his Sunday clothes. "I, uh, wanted to say goodbye."

For a moment Nathalie didn't know what to say. Then she remembered Lester falling down from exhaustion at the edge of Gold Creek, badly hurt, but still worried that she would see him without his clothes. Lester in the wheelbarrow; Lester being plucked. So much had happened.

"I'll miss you, Lester," replied Nathalie. "Who will help me roll the chalk?"

Lester smiled. "You were always so good at that kind of stuff. I was afraid I'd make a mistake and you'd laugh."

"I'd never laugh."

Lester put his hands in his pockets and seemed to become very interested in an ant that was making its way across Nathalie's front porch.

"You didn't tell."

"I promised I wouldn't. Anyway, Lester, it wasn't important. Not compared to everything else that happened. Anyway, you saw me in my curling rags. No lady likes to be seen in her curling rags!"

That got Lester laughing. "Yeah, your hair looks different now. You've got sausages instead of braids."

"They're not sausages! they're curls, silly. This is how I wear my hair now."

Oh," said Lester. The conversation slowed to a stop. Nathalie took a deep breath.

"Wait here, Lester. I've got something for you."

She ran to her room and took a small, splintered piece of wood from her dresser drawer. She ran back to Lester and shyly held it out to him.

"I want you to take this with you."

Lester looked confused. "What is it?"

"It's a piece of the railing from the little bridge that used to go over Gold Creek. You remember? I know it sounds stupid, but we, I mean Frances and Ruby and Abby and Jessie and me, we used to call it the wishing bridge. Every time we crossed, we made a wish. I loved that bridge," Nathalie added wistfully. Lester still looked confused.

"Anyway," Nathalie hurried on, "that night, I was crossing through the water just like you and I found this piece. I made a wish, and part of that wish was that you'd be safe. And just after I made the wish, I saw you. And now you're safe." Lester started to turn the piece of wood over and over in his hands.

"Will you take it, Lester? Maybe, if you hold it, it will help you think of me from time to time." Nathalie let out her breath, and dared herself to look at Lester's face.

"Sure, I'll take it." Lester looked back at Nathalie. "But I don't need a hunk of wood to help me remember you." Lester thrust something into Nathalie's hand. "This is so you don't forget me. Bye, Nathalie," he said, in a deeper voice than he usually had. Then he was gone.

Nathalie watched him until he was out of sight, her hand feeling a little tingly. Slowly she opened her fingers. In her palm lay a feather.

CHAPTER 28
One Last Wish

NATHALIE, LEFT ALONE IN FRANK, FELT AS though the world had ended. There were no more cinnamon whirligigs, no more games of Hull Gull or tiddlywinks. There were no more stories outside Andy's old tent. Nathalie sometimes wondered about Andy. Like Napi, he had created wonderful things – his stories – then disappeared. Maybe the two were together, telling stories and minding what was left of the mountain.

Charlie was gone too. Poor Charlie. He hadn't been hurt when the tunnels collapsed, but he'd got cut off from all the miners. When the miners got out, Charlie was left behind, trapped behind another wall of rock. But that didn't bother Charlie. He chewed on timbers and licked the droplets of water that ran down the walls of the tunnels, keeping himself alive underground for a whole month. When workers finally created a new opening to the mine, they found Charlie wandering around in the dark. Unfortunately, everyone was so happy to see him that they gave him too much to eat all at once, and that was the end of Charlie.

There wasn't much left for Nathalie and her mother in Frank. Nathalie's friends were gone, and it looked as though soon she might be gone too. Caroline had heard of a housekeeping position at a hotel in Lethbridge, and was thinking about moving the "Vaughan women" there. Nathalie didn't know how she felt about that. Frank wasn't a happy place to be, but it was the only home she knew.

Aunt Sadie and Helena had not come to visit. They could have come, for even though the train tracks hadn't been replaced, the CPR had arranged for a stage coach to take the passengers from the place where the tracks ended to where they began again. Aunt Sadie had chosen to take Helena back to Spokane.

Caroline had received a note from her sister saying that they had arrived home safely. There was no more talk of a visit. Nathalie guessed that it made sense for them to wait until rocks stopped falling from Turtle Mountain, but imagined that now they were too frightened to come. She sighed. The idea had just been too good to be true.

Just one thing in Frank was back to normal. The wishing bridge had been rebuilt over Gold Creek, once the floodwaters had gone down. Nathalie went there sometimes, as she had today, but she didn't know what to wish for. Sometimes she thought that her last wish had been so big that there simply weren't any more wishes left in her. But deep in her heart she thought that maybe she just didn't believe in wishes anymore. They seemed to work for some people some of the time, but wishing wasn't dependable. Most of the time she ended up disappointed. She was tired of being disappointed.

Nathalie was trying hard to see the brave, strong, smart girl that lived inside of her, just like Doc Malcolmson had said. Maybe strong girls didn't need wishes. Nathalie didn't know anymore. It was hard to feel brave and strong and smart when all you really felt was lonely.

Nathalie gazed deep into the water; there were many quiet pools now. She wished that the happy, gurgling water could still make its way away from Turtle Mountain, sparkling in the sun. But it was all dammed up. Everything was standing still. Nathalie looked up at the sun. It was getting late; she knew she should go home for supper.

Nathalie walked along the path to town until she came to Dominion Avenue. As she was turning left to go to her house, she happened to glance to the right.

The CPR stagecoach had just arrived. Three strangers climbed out, and Nathalie watched them curiously. There was a woman about her mother's age, a little girl with long curls, and a very old man. They didn't belong in Frank. They didn't fit. The only strangers coming to Frank these days were mining engineers, coming to check what was left of Turtle Mountain. These three didn't look like engineers. All of a sudden, Nathalie realized who they were, gasped, then turned and ran.

She raced back to her house. Her mother looked up with alarm.

"Nathalie, what on earth's the matter? You look like you've seen a ghost!"

Nathalie tried to catch her breath. "Mama, they're here, they came! They're here right now!"

"Who's here, sweetheart?"

"Grandfather's come."

Her mother went white. "How do you know?"

"I saw them. They were getting off the stagecoach. Helena still has long curls! And there was an old man. It was Grandfather, it had to be! Why, Mama? Why? Why are they here? How come you didn't tell me?"

"I didn't know, Nathalie. They didn't let me know they were coming."

Caroline reached for Nathalie's hand, as if for support, and the two of them sat together on the sofa. "Why did they come, Mama? Don't they know we're moving to Lethbridge?"

"Hush, child," said Caroline. "Yes, I did write to Sadie and tell her we were moving. So I don't know why they're here. We shall have to wait and see. Why don't you put on a kettle?"

Nathalie had just started for the kitchen when she heard the knock at the door. She froze. There they were, standing there, all three of them. Nobody said a word. Then Grandfather said, in a voice unlike the one in Nathalie's dreams, "Caroline, may I come in?"

Nathalie's mother nodded her head. Grandfather came into the sitting room and sat in their best chair. Aunt Sadie was smiling. Nathalie thought that she looked like a nice person, but still felt nervous. She peeked over at Helena. She was so beautiful! But Helena looked as nervous as Nathalie felt.

Why were they here?

Nathalie's mother motioned for her to come close. "Father, this is my daughter, Nathalie. You may not remember her."

Nathalie tried to stand as straight as possible. Brave, strong, smart. Brave, strong, smart. She said the words over and over in her head, but still the pressure began to build behind her eyes. What would he see? Would he be disappointed in her? Again?

To Nathalie's surprise, a tear rolled down her Grandfather's cheek. "I have been a foolish old man," he said quietly. "Please forgive me."

That single tear opened the floodgates, or at least it seemed that way to Nathalie. In moments, everyone was crying, and explaining, and apologizing. Was this really the man she had been afraid of all her life? And could she forgive him just like that? Forgive him all her nightmares, and the years of hurt in her mother's eyes? Nathalie backed away in bewilderment. And bumped into Helena.

The two girls looked at one another, the one in pigtails and mended stockings, the other in curls and patent leather shoes. "Do you want to go outside?" Nathalie asked shyly. "It sounds like they have a lot to talk about."

"I'd like that," replied Helena. "I hate it when Grandfather cries."

Nathalie was astounded. "Does he cry a lot?"

"Only when he talks about your mother. He always talks about his 'terrible mistake' and then he cries. One day I asked him why he didn't just say he was sorry, but he got mad at me, so I never asked him again. Grown-ups are very strange, you know."

Nathalie smiled. She wasn't yet sure about her grandfather, but she was certain she was going to like Helena. "Would you like to see our wishing bridge?" she asked.

"You have a wishing bridge? I make a wish every night before I go to sleep. But they don't all come true. Do yours?"

"Sometimes they do. Like today." Helena smiled. The two girls joined hands and ran towards Gold Creek, feeling the wind in their hair.

Dominion Avenue in Frank before the slide, with Turtle Mountain in the background. Glenbow Archives NA-3011-2.

AUTHOR'S NOTE

To find out more about life in Frank at the turn of the century, I talked to people whose families had lived in the area for a long time; I read books and newspaper articles; I found songs and stories. These resources help us to understand and remember the Frank Slide.

THE PEOPLE OF FRANK

Mining jobs drew immigrants from many parts of the world, bringing rich cultural traditions to the area. A good job may be the reason why Nathalie's father came north. At the time of the slide, there were about six hundred people living in Frank.

Many of the characters in this book were real people. Frances Bansemer, Jessie Leitch, Ruby Watkins, Lester Johnson, and their families all lived in the row of miners' cabins on "the field side." The real Lester did indeed make his way out of his crushed house and all the way to the Williamsons' cabin with the feathery stake in his side. Andy Grissack, Lillian Clark, and the Thornleys all lived past the wishing bridge as well. William Warrington did, sadly, lose his family in the disaster. In all, seventy-six people are known to have died, although only twelve bodies were ever recovered. The rest still lay under the rocks.

Joseph Chapman, Dan McKenzie, Evan Jones, William Warrington, Alex Grant, "Shorty" Dawson, Alex McPhail, John Watkins, and Charles Farrell took fourteen hours to dig themselves out from under the slide. The names of the eight other miners who were with them have been lost to history.

Baby Marion became the most famous survivor of the slide. Many stories were told and songs were sung about the baby everyone called "Frankie Slide," the baby who was plucked from the rocks by one of the rescuers.

Most of the games Nathalie and her friends played are familiar today: cards, checkers, dolls and dollhouses, jacks, jigsaw puzzles, jump rope, slingshots, tiddly-

View of in Frank after the slide. Glenbow Archives NA-411-9.

winks, tops, tangrams, paper dolls, and hopscotch. Others, like "My Grandfather's General Store" are less familiar.

For examples of turn-of-the-century games and how to play them (including the rules for "Hull Gull") visit: http://www.emporia.edu/cgps/tales/m95tales.htm.

ROCK SLIDES

Rock slides usually occur without warning, and happen very quickly. But they cause terrible damage to both the environment and to the people who live nearby. A slide is considered a disaster in Canada if it results in three or more deaths. In the last 160 years,

The Bansemer house the morning after the slide. Glenbow Archives NA-586-2.

there have been forty-three slide disasters in Canada, killing 570 people. The Frank Slide accounts for seventy-six of those deaths, and is on record as Canada's worst slide disaster.

No single theory of the cause of the slide has ever been accepted, but there are many ideas. Turtle Mountain had always been prone to movement because of its unstable structure. The mining tunnels made Turtle Mountain even weaker. But the unseasonably cold weather was also part of the problem.

Warm weather in the days before the slide had allowed water to seep into cracks. Some of the cracks were caused by the blasting and some were part of the mountain's structure. When the temperature suddenly dropped, the water froze and expanded, breaking huge chunks of rock off the mountain, contributing to the disaster.

The slide only lasted 90 seconds, but filled the valley to a depth of 100 feet with rocks and mud. Some of the rocks were carried away to clear the railway tracks. That took three weeks. Some of the rocks were blasted away to make a road. That took three years. Today, more than a hundred years later, the rest of the rocks lie just where they fell in 1903.

To find out more about rockslides, visit the "School of Rock" at Canadian Geographic's Kids Atlas Online for slide shows, videos, games and quizzes about the rocks that make up Earth. http://www.canadiangeographic.ca/cgKidsAtlas/rock.asp.

THE BLACKFOOT STORYTELLERS

The people of the Blackfoot lived in the Crowsnest Pass. That was the name for the part of the North-West Territories that included the town of Frank. (The area became Alberta in 1905.) Some say the Crowsnest Pass was named in honour of a great battle. The Blackfoot fought the Crow Nation of Montana at the foot of Turtle Mountain. During the battle, a big piece of the mountain fell, killing many Crow warriors. Both Nations called a truce, and agreed not to break the peace.

But that's just one story. Some say the area was home to many big, black crows.

Andy's story of Napi and the Spirit Wife is called a creation myth. It's really two stories in one. The first part is the story of the Spirit Wife falling from the sky. It is a very old story told not just by the Blackfoot, but also by the Iroquois, the Seneca, the Cherokee, the Tikigaq and the Algonquin. Variations are also told in lots of other places like Japan, Finland, and Siberia. In all of the stories, spirits live in the sky and one comes down to earth (often by accident) to help finish creating the earth.

The second part is the story of Napi creating all of earth's creatures. It is not quite so old and is also told by people all over the world, although different cultures use different names for Napi.

Storytellers don't always agree on the details of these stories. Some Blackfoot storytellers say that Napi himself was the one who fell, and that it was he who asked the creatures to find the earth to put on turtle's back. Some tellers don't believe that the Spirit Wife was Napi's mother; in fact, they don't believe that he had a mother. They think that the Spirit Wife fell down and asked the Swimmers to finish the earth, then went back to the sky, and Napi came later from the south, walking all the way to Turtle Mountain, creating animals and people as he went. Some say that when Napi was done, he went back to the Sky; some say he went under the earth; some say he went into a mountain.

The storyteller can change the details, but the end of the story is always the same. Napi creates all the creatures of the earth, including man and woman. Together, the two stories are called "The Earth Diver Story."

The history books tell us that Chief Running Wolf told the people of Frank many times that the mountain was moving, to warn them about the dangers of mining Turtle Mountain.

To learn more about the Blackfoot People visit "Niitsitapiisini: Our Way of Life." This interactive site explores the Blackfoot culture of the past and the present. You can even listen to stories about Napi in the Blackfoot language. http://www.glenbow.org/blackfoot/index.htm.

THE CANADIAN PACIFIC RAILWAY

The CPR opened the tracks through the Crowsnest Pass in 1898. The line was built to help develop the coal industry. It was also built to make sure that the line remained Canadian. At the time, American companies were very interested in building their own lines into Canada so they could ship silver, copper, lead, and zinc to the south.

It was expensive to build the line, so the CPR asked the government to help. In exchange, the government

Passengers standing by the Spokane Flyer, after it was flagged down and saved from danger. Glenbow Archives NA-3437-11.

said that the CPR had to charge very low rates for the freight the trains carried. This low rate was known as "The Crow Rate."

Sid Choquette did stop the Spokane Flyer, saving many lives, and he and his partner Lowes were given $25.00 cheques for their heroism.

For more on the history of the Canadian Pacific Railway, check out: http://www.virtualmuseum.ca/PM.cgi?LM=Games&LANG=English&AP=vmc_search&scope=Games, website of the Virtual Museum of Canada. Scroll down to "The Adventure Train!" game to start traveling the country by rail.

Sightseers came from far away to view the Frank Slide. This is just one of the boulders that tumbled down the mountainside. Glenbow Archives NA-3437-11

COAL MINING

In 1873, Michael Phillipps discovered rich coal seams in the Crowsnest Pass while searching for gold. Coal was a very valuable product, needed to heat homes, provide electricity, fuel steam locomotives, and make steel.

When the Canadian Pacific Railway put tracks through the Crowsnest Pass, a dozen coal mines sprang up in the area. The trains provided a way to get the coal to market. Towns like Frank were built around the mines so that the miners would have a place to live.

But coal mining was very dangerous – there were many accidents and explosions. The worst local explosion was the Hillcrest Mine Disaster on June 19, 1914, which killed 189 men.

The miners used lamps to light their way when they were underground. Each miner would pick up a lamp from the lamp room before going on shift and return it at the end of the shift. If all the lamps were not returned, the workers of the next shift knew that there was a problem and a search would be organized.

The Frank Mine was reopened after the slide, but closed permanently in 1918. Today, it is possible to get a sense of the life of a coal miner by putting on a head lamp and visiting the underground coal mine at Bellevue, Alberta.

To test your mining know-how or try out a miner's maze, visit: http://www.coalminer.ca/miniminers/mini_miners.asp.

The bridge still stretches over Gold Creek. I made a wish there once myself. Although Nathalie lives only in my imagination, I hope that someday all of her wishes will come true.

ACKNOWLEDGEMENTS

My sincere thanks to those who helped this book come to life: Pat Carfra, who had the idea. Robert Perry, Lise Henderson, and Kate Lord, who shared their thoughts. Monica Field, Christa Peters, Diane Peterson, and Kristin Kovach of the Frank Slide Interpretive Centre, who filled in the details. Barbara Sapergia, who helped it grow.

And my husband Dale, who made it possible.

Penny Draper

BIBLIOGRAPHY

Anderson, Frank, *The Frank Slide Story*. Calgary: Frontiers Unlimited, 1961.

Cochrane, Jean, *The One-Room School in Canada*. Fitzhenry and Whiteside, 2001.

Kerr, J. William, *Frank Slide*. Calgary: Barker Publishing Ltd., 1990.

Looker, Janet, *Disaster Canada*. Lynx Images, 2000.

Yackulic, George A., "The Slide That Shook the West," in *In the Face of Disaster; True Stories of Canadian Heroisms* from the Archives of *Maclean's*, Introduction by Peter C. Newman. Rogers Media, 2000.

The Frank Slide Interpretive Centre, archival material. Blairmore, Crowsnest Pass, Alberta. http://www.frankslide.com

Geological Survey of Canada, Stephen G. Evans. http://www.cseg.ca/conferences/2000/2000abstracts/1072.PDF

The Crowsnest Pass Railway Route. Website of the Canadian Museum of Rail Travel, Cranbrook BC. http://www.crowsnest.bc.ca/

Hurt, Les, "When Coal Was King, Coal Mining in Western Canada," extracted from the *Bibliography of the Crowsnest Pass* (Unpublished Report: Historic Sites Service, Alberta Community Development, no date). Reprinted with permission on: http://www.coalking.ca/industry/railways.html

Taped pioneer interview of Jean Reid; resident of Frank from 1912 to 1922. Conducted for the *Crowsnest Pass History Book.*

ABOUT THE AUTHOR

PENNY DRAPER HAS BEEN ENTRANCED by stories all of her life. When she was little, her most prized possession was a flashlight, which she used to read under the covers long after lights out. Her mother said she ate books.

Penny received a Bachelor's Degree in Literature from Trinity College, University of Toronto, and on the side, attended the Storytellers' School of Toronto. Inspired by this experience, Penny began the Prince George Storytellers Roundtable, a dynamic group of storytellers dedicated to promoting the oral tradition throughout northern British Columbia, where she lived.

For the next fifteen years, Penny shared tales as a professional storyteller at schools, libraries, parks, castles, universities, educational conferences, festivals, and on radio and television. She has told stories in an Arabian harem and from inside a bear's belly – but that is a story in itself.

Penny is currently a freelance writer and reviewer with articles in newspapers and magazines. She also works at the University of Victoria.

In the bookstore, of course.

Also available from Coteau Books

FROM MANY PEOPLES

CHRISTMAS AT WAPOS BAY
by Jordan Wheeler & Dennis Jackson

At Christmas time in Northern Saskatchewan, three Cree children –
Talon, Raven, and T-Bear – visit their *Moshum's* (Grandfather's) cabin
to learn about traditional ways and experience a life-changing adventure.
ISBN 13: 978-1-55050-324-1   ISBN 10: 1-55050-324-3 $8.95

NETTIE'S JOURNEY
by Adele Dueck

Nettie's story of life in a Mennonite village in Ukraine as told to her granddaughter
in present-day Saskatchewan. From the dangers of WWI to their escape to Canada,
this is a captivating eye-witness account of a turbulent period in history.
ISBN 13: 978-1-55050-322-7   ISBN 10: 1-55050-322-7 $8.95

ADELINE'S DREAM
by Linda Aksomitis

Adeline has to struggle to make a place for herself when she comes
to Canada from Germany one spring. Life in her new home is definitely dramatic,
but by Christmas time she starts to feel a sense of belonging in her new home.
ISBN 13: 978-1-55050-323-4   ISBN 10: 1-55050-323-5 $8.95

THE SECRET OF THE STONE HOUSE
by Judith Silverthorne

Twelve-year-old Emily Bradford travels back in time to witness
her ancestors pioneering in Saskatchewan and discovers a secret
that will help explore her family's roots in Scotland.
ISBN 13: 978-1-55050-325-8   ISBN 10: 1-55050-325-1 $8.95

Available at fine bookstores everywhere.

Amazing Stories. Amazing Kids.

WWW.COTEAUBOOKS.COM